"I will not
said

"Come spring, I will rejoin Grom Hellscream, and help his noble clan storm the camps and free our people."

"Grom Hellscream," sneered the stranger, waving his hand dismissively. "A demon-ridden dreamer. I have seen what the humans can do, and it is best to avoid them."

"I was raised by humans, and believe me, they are not infallible!" cried Thrall. "Nor are you, I would think, you coward!"

"Thrall—" began Drek'Thar, speaking up at last.

"No, Master Drek'Thar, I will not be silent. This stranger comes seeking our aid, eats at our fire, and dares to insult the courage of our clan and his own race. I will not stand for it. I am not the chieftain, nor do I claim that right. But I will claim my right to fight this stranger, and make him eat his words sliced upon my sword."

The strange orc laughed heartily and rose. He was almost as big as Thrall, and now, to his astonishment, Thrall saw that this arrogant stranger was completely clad in black plate armor, trimmed with brass. Uttering a fierce cry, the stranger opened his pack and pulled out the largest warhammer Thrall had ever seen. He held it aloft with seeming ease, then brandished it at Thrall.

"See if you can take me, whelp!"

WarCraft

LORD OF
THE CLANS

CHRISTIE GOLDEN

POCKET BOOKS
New York   London   Toronto   Sydney

This book is a work of fiction. Names, characters, places and incidents are products of the author's imagination or are used fictitiously. Any resemblance to actual events or locales or persons living or dead is entirely coincidental.

An *Original* Publication of POCKET BOOKS

POCKET BOOKS, a division of Simon & Schuster, Inc.
1230 Avenue of the Americas, New York, NY 10020

© 2001 by Blizzard Entertainment. All rights reserved. Warcraft and Blizzard Entertainment are trademarks or registered trademarks of Blizzard Entertainment in the U.S. and/or other countries. All other trademarks are the property of their respective owners.

All rights reserved, including the right to reproduce this book or portions thereof in any form whatsoever. For information address Pocket Books, 1230 Avenue of the Americas, New York, NY 10020
ISBN 13: 978-0-7434-2690-9
ISBN 10:   0-7434-2690-8
First Pocket Books printing October 2001

20 19 18 17 16 15 14

POCKET and colophon are registered trademarks of Simon & Schuster, Inc.

For information regarding special discounts for bulk purchases, please contact Simon & Schuster Special Sales at 1-800-456-6798 or business@simonandschuster.com

Cover art by Sam Didier

Printed in the U.S.A.

This book is dedicated to its "holy trinity":

Lucienne Diver
Jessica McGivney
and
Chris Metzen

with appreciation for their enthusiastic support
and unwavering faith in my work.

LORD OF
THE CLANS

PROLOGUE

They came when Gul'dan called them, those who had willingly—*nay, eagerly*—sold their souls to the darkness. Once they, like Gul'dan, had been deeply spiritual beings. Once, they had studied the natural world and the orcs' place in it; had learned from the beasts of forest and field, the birds of the air, the fish of the rivers and oceans. And they had been a part of that cycle, no more, no less.

No longer.

These former shamans, these new warlocks, had had the briefest taste of power and, like the barest drop of honey on the tongue, found it sweet indeed. So their eagerness had been rewarded with more power, and still more. Gul'dan himself had learned from his master Ner'zhul until student had finally surpassed teacher. While it had been because of Ner'zhul that the Horde had become the powerful, unstoppable tide of destruction it presently was, Ner'zhul had not had the courage to go further. He had a soft spot for the inherent nobility of his people. Gul'dan had no such weakness.

The Horde had slain all there was to slay in this world. They were lost with no outlet for their bloodlust, and were turning on one another, clan attacking clan in a desperate attempt to assuage the brutal longings that flamed in their hearts. It was Gul'dan who had found a fresh target upon which to focus the Horde's white-hot need to slaughter. Now they would soon venture into a new world, filled with fresh, easy, unsuspecting prey. The bloodlust would rise to a fever pitch, and the wild Horde needed a council to guide them. Gul'dan would lead that council.

He nodded to them as they entered, his small, fire-hazed eyes missing nothing. One by one they came, called like servile beasts to their master. To him.

They sat around the table, the most feared, revered, and loathed among the entire orcish clans. Some were hideous, having paid the price for their dark knowledge with more than just their souls. Others were yet fair, their bodies whole and strong with smooth green skin stretched tight across rippling muscles. Such had been their request in the dark bargain. All were ruthless, cunning, and would stop at nothing to gain more power.

But none was as ruthless as Gul'dan.

"We few gathered here," began Gul'dan in his raspy voice, "are the mightiest of our clans. We know power. How to get it, how to use it, and how to get more. Others are beginning to speak out against one or the other of us. This clan wishes to return to its roots; that clan is tired of killing defenseless infants." His thick green lips curled into a sneer of contempt. "This is what happens when orcs go soft."

"But, Great One," one of the warlocks said, "we have slain all the Draenei. What is there left to kill in this world?"

Gul'dan smiled, stretching his thick lips over large, sharp teeth. "Nothing," he said. "But other worlds await."

He told them of the plan, taking pleasure in the lust for power that was kindled in their red eyes. Yes, this would be good. This would be the most powerful organization of orcs that had ever existed, and at the head of this organization would be none other than Gul'dan.

"And we will be the council that makes the Horde dance to our tune," he said at last. "Each one of us is a powerful voice. Yet such is the orcish pride that they must not know who is truly the master here. Let each think that he swings his battle-ax because he wills it, not because we are commanding it. We will stay a secret. We are the walkers in the shadows, the power that is all the more potent for its invisibility. We are the Shadow Council, and none shall know of our strength."

Yet, one day, and that day soon, some would know.

ONE

E ven the beasts were cold on a night such as this, mused Durotan. Absently he reached out to his wolf companion and scratched Sharptooth behind one of his white ears. The animal crooned appreciatively and snuggled closer. Wolf and orc chief stared together at the silent fall of white snow, framed by the rough oval that was the entrance to Durotan's cave.

Once, Durotan, chieftain of the Frostwolf clan, had known the kiss of balmier climes. Had swung his ax in the sunlight, narrowing small eyes against the gleam of sunshine on metal and against the spattering of red human blood. Once, he had felt a kinship with all of his people, not just those of his clan. Side by side they had stood, a green tide of death flooding over the hillsides to engulf the humans. They had feasted at the fires together, laughed their deep, booming laughs, told the stories of blood and conquest while their children drowsed by the dying embers, their little minds filled with images of slaughter.

But now the handful of orcs that comprised the Frostwolf clan shivered alone in their exile in the frigid Alterac Mountains of this alien world. Their only friends here were the huge white wolves. They were so different from the mammoth black wolves that Durotan's people had once ridden, but a wolf was a wolf, no matter the color of its fur, and determined patience combined with Drek'Thar's powers had won the beasts over to them. Now orc and wolf hunted together and kept one another warm during the interminable, snowy nights.

A soft, snuffling sound from the heart of the cave caused Durotan to turn. His harsh face, lined and held in perpetual tautness from years of worry and anger, softened at the noise. His little son, as yet unnamed until the ordained Naming Day of this cycle, had cried out as he was being fed.

Leaving Sharptooth to continue watching the snowfall, Durotan rose and lumbered back to the cave's inner chamber. Draka had bared a breast for the child to suckle upon, and had just removed the infant from his task. So that was why the child had whimpered. As Durotan watched, Draka extended a forefinger. With a black nail honed to razor sharpness, she pricked deep into the nipple before returning the infant's small head to her breast. Not a flicker of pain crossed her beautiful, strong-jawed face. Now, as the child fed, he would drink not only nourishing mother's milk, but his mother's blood as well. Such was appropriate food for a budding young warrior, the son of Durotan, the future chieftain of the Frostwolves.

His heart swelled with love for his mate, a warrior his equal in courage and cunning, and the lovely, perfect son they had borne.

It was then that the knowledge of what he had to do sank over him, like a blanket settling over his shoulders. He sat down and sighed deeply.

Draka glanced up at him, her brown eyes narrowing. She knew him all too well. He did not want to tell her of his sudden decision, although he knew in his heart it was the right one. But he must.

"We have a child now," Durotan said, his deep voice booming from his broad chest.

"Yes," replied Draka, pride in her voice. "A fine, strong son, who will lead the Frostwolf clan after his father dies nobly in battle. Many years from now," she added.

"I have a responsibility for his future," Durotan continued.

Draka's attention was now on him fully. He thought her exquisitely beautiful at this moment, and tried to brand the image of her in his mind. The firelight played against her green skin, casting her powerful muscles into sharp relief and making her tusks gleam. She did not interrupt, merely waited for him to continue.

"Had I not spoken against Gul'dan, our son would

have more playmates with which to grow up," Durotan continued. "Had I not spoken against Gul'dan, we would have continued to be valued members of the Horde."

Draka hissed, opening her massive jaws and baring her fangs in displeasure at her mate. "You would not have been the mate I joined with," she boomed. The infant, startled, jerked his head away from the nourishing breast to look up at his mother's face. White milk and red blood dripped down his already jutting chin. "Durotan of the Frostwolf clan would not sit by and meekly let our people be led to their deaths like the sheep the humans tend. With what you had learned, you had to speak out, my mate. You could have done no less and still be the chieftain you are."

Durotan nodded at the truth of her words. "To know that Gul'dan had no love for our people, that it was nothing more than a way for him to increase his power. . . ."

He fell silent, recalling the shock and horror—and rage—that had engulfed him when he had learned of the Shadow Council and Gul'dan's duplicity. He had tried to convince the others of the danger facing them all. They had been used, like pawns, to destroy the Draenei, a race that Durotan was beginning to think had not required extinction after all. And again, shuttled through the Dark Portal onto an unsuspecting world—not the orcs' decision, no, but that of the Shadow Council. All for Gul'dan, all for Gul'dan's personal power. How many orcs had fallen, fighting for something so empty?

He searched for the words to express his decision to his mate. "I spoke, and we were exiled. All who followed me were. It is a great dishonor."

"Only Gul'dan's dishonor," said Draka fiercely. The infant had gotten over his temporary fright and was again nursing. "Your people are alive, and free, Durotan. It is a harsh place, but we have found the frost wolves to be our companions. We have plenty of fresh meat, even in the depths of winter. We have kept the old ways alive, as much as we can, and the stories around the fire are part of our children's heritage."

"They deserve more," said Durotan. He gestured with a sharp-nailed finger at his suckling son. "He deserves more. Our still-deluded brothers deserve more. And I will give it to them."

He rose and straightened to his full imposing height. His huge shadow fell over the forms of his wife and child. Her crestfallen expression told him that Draka knew what he was going to say before he spoke, but the words needed utterance. It was what made them solid, real . . . made them an oath not to be broken.

"There were some who heeded me, though they still doubted. I will return and find those few chieftains. I will convince them of the truth of my story, and they will rally their people. We shall no longer be slaves of Gul'dan, easily lost and not thought of when we die in battles that serve only him. This I swear, I, Durotan, chieftain of the Frostwolf clan!"

He threw back his head, opened his toothy mouth almost impossibly wide, rolled his eyes back, and uttered a loud, deep, furious cry. The baby began to squall and even Draka flinched. It was the Oath Cry, and he knew that despite the deep snow that often deadened sound, everyone in his clan would hear it this night. In moments, they would cluster around his cave, demanding to know the content of the Oath Cry, and making cries of their own.

"You shall not go alone, my mate," said Draka, her soft voice a sharp contrast to the ear-splitting sound of Durotan's Oath Cry. "We shall come with you."

"I forbid it."

And with a suddenness that startled even Durotan, who ought to have known better, Draka sprang to her feet. The crying baby tumbled from her lap as she clenched her fists and raised them, shaking them violently. A heartbeat later Durotan blinked as pain shot through him and blood dripped down his face. She had bounded the length of the cave and slashed his cheek with her nails.

"I am Draka, daughter of Kelkar, son of Rhakish. No one forbids me to follow my mate, not even Durotan himself! I come with you, I stand by you, I shall die if need be. Pagh!" She spat at him.

As he wiped the mixture of spittle and blood from his face, his heart swelled with love for this female. He had been right to choose her as his mate, to be the mother of his sons. Was there ever a more fortunate male in all of orc history? He did not think so.

Despite the fact that, if word reached Gul'dan, Orgrim Doomhammer and his clan would be exiled, the great Warchief made Durotan and his family welcome in his field camp. The wolf, however, he eyed with suspicion. The wolf eyed him back in the same manner. The rough tent that served Doomhammer for shelter was emptied of lesser orcs, and Durotan, Draka, and their yet-unnamed child were ushered in.

The night was a bit cool to Doomhammer, and he watched with wry amusement as his honored guests divested themselves of most of their clothing and muttered about the heat. Frostwolves, he mused, must be unused to such "warm weather."

Outside, his personal guards kept watch. With the flap that served as a door still open, Doomhammer watched them huddle around the fire, extending enormous green hands to the dancing flames. The night was dark, save for the small lights of the stars. Durotan had picked a good night for his clandestine visit. It was unlikely that the small party of male, female, and child had been spotted and identified for who they really were.

"I regret that I place you and your clan in jeopardy," were the first words Durotan spoke.

Doomhammer waved the comment aside. "If Death

is to come for us, it will find us behaving with honor."
He invited them to sit and with his own hands handed
his old friend the dripping haunch of a fresh kill. It was
still warm. Durotan nodded his acceptance, bit into the
juicy flesh, and tore off a huge chunk. Draka did likewise, and then extended her bloody fingers to her baby.
The child eagerly sucked the sweet liquid.

"A fine, strong boy," said Doomhammer.

Durotan nodded. "He will be a fitting leader of my
clan. But we did not come all this way for you to ad-
mire my son."

"You spoke with veiled words many years ago," said
Doomhammer.

"I wished to protect my clan, and I was not certain
my suspicions were correct until Gul'dan imposed the
exile," Durotan replied. "His swift punishment made it
clear that what I knew was true. Listen, my old friend,
and then you must judge for yourself."

In soft tones, so that the guards sitting at the fire a
few yards away would not overhear them, Durotan
began to speak. He told Doomhammer everything he
knew—the bargain with the demon lord, the obscene
nature of Gul'dan's power, the betrayal of the clans
through the Shadow Council, the eventual, and dishonorable, end of the orcs, who would be thrown as bait to
demonic forces. Doomhammer listened, forcing his
wide face to remain impassive. But within his broad
chest his heart pounded like his own famous warhammer upon human flesh.

Could this be true? It sounded like a tale spewed by a battle-addled half-wit. Demons, dark pacts . . . and yet, this was Durotan who was speaking. Durotan, who was one of the wisest, fiercest, and noblest of the chieftains. From any other mouth, these he would have judged to be lies or nonsense. But Durotan had been exiled for his words, which lent them credence. And Doomhammer had trusted the other chieftain with his life many times before now.

There was only one conclusion. What Durotan was telling him was true. When his old friend finished speaking, Doomhammer reached for the meat and took another bite, chewing slowly while his racing mind tried to make sense of all that had been said. Finally, he swallowed, and spoke.

"I believe you, old friend. And let me reassure you, I will not stand for Gul'dan's plans for our people. We will stand against the darkness with you."

Obviously moved, Durotan extended his hand. Doomhammer gripped it tightly.

"You cannot stay overlong in this camp, though it would be an honor to have you do so," Doomhammer said as he rose. "One of my personal guards will escort you to a safe place. There is a stream nearby and much game in the woods this time of year, so you shall not go hungry. I will do what I can on your behalf, and when the time is right, you and I shall stand side by side as we slay the Great Betrayer Gul'dan together."

* * *

The guard said nothing as he led them out of the encampment several miles into the surrounding woods. Sure enough, the clearing to which he took them was secluded and verdant. Durotan could hear the trickling of the water. He turned to Draka.

"I knew my old friend could be trusted," he said. "It will not be long before—"

And then Durotan froze. He had heard another noise over the splashing of the nearby stream. It was the snap of a twig under a heavy foot. . . .

He screamed his battle cry and reached for his ax. Before he could even grasp the hilt the assassins were upon him. Dimly, Durotan heard Draka's shrill scream of rage, but could spare no instant to turn to her aid. Out of the corner of his eye, he saw Sharptooth spring on one intruder, knocking him to the earth.

They had come silently, with none of the pride in the hunt that was so integral to orcish honor. These were assassins, the lowest of the low, the worm beneath the foot. Except these worms were everywhere, and though their mouths remained closed in that unnatural silence, their weapons spoke with a purposeful tongue.

An ax bit deep into Durotan's left thigh and he fell. Warm blood flowed down his leg as he twisted and reached with his bare hands, trying desperately to throttle his would-be murderer. He stared up into a face frighteningly devoid of good, honest orc rage, indeed of any emotion at all. His adversary lifted the ax again. With every ounce of strength left to him,

Durotan's hands closed on the orc's throat. Now the worm did show emotion as he dropped the ax, trying to pry Durotan's thick, powerful fingers from his neck.

A brief, sharp howl, then silence. Sharptooth had fallen. Durotan did not need to look to see. He still heard his mate grunting obscenities at the orc who, he knew, would slay her. And then a noise that sent fear shivering through him split the air: his infant son's cry of terror.

They shall not kill my son! The thought gave Durotan new strength and with a roar, despite the lifeblood ebbing from the severed artery in his leg, he surged upward and managed to get his foe beneath his huge bulk. Now the assassin squirmed in genuine terror. Durotan pressed hard with both hands and felt the satisfying snap of neck beneath his palms.

"No!" The voice belonged to the treasonous guard, the orc who had betrayed them. It was high, humanish with fear. "No, I'm one of you, they are the target—"

Durotan looked up in time to see a huge assassin swing a blade almost bigger than he was in a smooth, precise arc. Doomhammer's personal guard didn't stand a chance. The sword sliced cleanly through the traitor's neck, and as the severed, bloody head flew past him, Durotan could still see the shock and surprise on the dead guard's face.

He turned to defend his mate, but he was too late. Durotan cried aloud in fury and raw grief as he saw Draka's still body, hacked almost to pieces, lying on the forest floor in a widening pool of blood. Her killer loomed over her, and now turned his attention to Durotan.

In a fair battle, Durotan would have been a match for any three of them. Grievously wounded as he was, with no weapon save his hands, he knew he was about to die. He did not try to defend himself. Instead, out of deep instinct he reached for the small bundle that was his child.

And stared foolishly at the spurting fountain of blood that sprang from his shoulder. His reflexes were slowing from lack of blood, and before he could even react, his left arm joined the right to lie, twitching, on the ground. The worms would not even let him hold his son one more time.

The injured leg could bear him no longer. Durotan toppled forward. His face was inches away from that of his son's. His mighty warrior's heart broke at the expression on the baby's face, an expression of total confusion and terror.

"Take . . . the child," he rasped, amazed that he could even speak.

The assassin bent close, so that Durotan could see him. He spat in Durotan's eye. For a moment, Durotan feared he would impale the baby right in front of his father's eyes.

"We will leave the child for the forest creatures," snarled the assassin. "Perhaps you can watch as they tear him to bits."

And then they were gone, as silently as they had left.

Durotan blinked, feeling dazed and disoriented as the blood left his body in rivers. He tried again to move and could not. He could only stare with failing eyesight at the image of his son, his small chest heaving with his screams, his tiny fists balled and waving frantically.

Draka . . . my beloved . . . my little son . . . I am so sorry. I have brought us to this. . . .

The edges of his vision began to turn gray. The image of his child began to fade. The only comfort that Durotan, chieftain of the Frostwolf clan, had as his life slowly ebbed from him was the knowledge that he would die before having to witness the horrible spectacle of his son being eaten alive by ravenous forest beasts.

"By the Light, what a noise!" Twenty-two-year-old Tammis Foxton wrinkled his nose at the noise that was echoing through the forest. "Might as well turn back, Lieutenant. Anything that loud is certain to have frightened any game worth pursuing."

Lieutenant Aedelas Blackmoore threw his personal servant a lazy grin.

"Haven't you learned anything I've tried to teach you, Tammis?" he drawled. "It's as much about getting away from that damned fortress as bringing back supper. Let whatever it is caterwaul all it likes." He reached for the saddlebag behind him. The bottle felt cool and smooth in his hand.

"Hunting cup, sir?" Tammis, despite Blackmoore's comments, had been ideally trained. He extended a small cup in the shape of a dragon's head that had been hooked onto his saddle. Hunting cups were specifically designed for such a purpose, having no base upon which to sit. Blackmoore debated, then waved the offer away.

"One too many steps." With his teeth he pulled out the cork, held it in one hand, and raised the bottle's mouth to his lips.

Ah, this stuff was sweet. It burned an easy trail down his throat and into his gut. Wiping his mouth, Blackmoore recorked the bottle and put it back in the saddlebag. He deliberately ignored Tammis's look, quickly averted, of concern. What should a servant care how much his master drank?

Aedelas Blackmoore had risen swiftly through the ranks because of his almost incredible ability to slice a swath through the ranks of orcs on the battlefield. His superiors thought this due to skill and courage. Blackmoore could have told them that his courage was of the liquid variety, but he didn't see much point in it.

His reputation also didn't hurt his chances with the ladies. Neither did his dashing good looks. Tall and handsome, with black hair that fell to his shoulders, steel-blue eyes, and a small, neatly trimmed goatee, he was the perfect heroic soldier. If some of the women left his bed a little sadder but wiser, and more than occasionally with a bruise or two, it mattered nothing to him. There were always plenty more where they came from.

The ear-splitting sound was starting to irritate him. "It's not going away," Blackmoore growled.

"It could be an injured creature, sir, incapable of crawling away," said Tammis.

"Then let's find it and put it out of our misery," replied Blackmoore. He kicked Nightsong, a sleek gelding as black as his name, with more force than was necessary and took off at a gallop in the direction of the hellish noise.

Nightsong came to such an abrupt halt that Blackmoore, usually the finest of riders, nearly sailed over the beast's head. He swore and punched the animal in the neck, then fell silent as he saw what had caused Nightsong to stop so quickly.

"Blessed Light," said Tammis, riding up beside him on his small gray pony. "What a mess."

Three orcs and a huge white wolf lay sprawled on the forest floor. Blackmoore assumed that they had died recently. There was as yet no stink of decomposition, though the blood had congealed. Two males, one female. Who cared what sex the wolf had been. Damned orcs. It would save humans like him a lot of trouble if the brutes turned on themselves more often.

Something moved, and Blackmoore saw what it was that had been shrieking so violently. It was the ugliest thing he had ever seen . . . an orc baby, wrapped in what no doubt passed for a swaddling cloth among the creatures. Staring, he dismounted and went to it.

"Careful, sir!" yelped Tammis. "It might bite!"

"I've never seen a whelp before," said Blackmoore. He nudged it with his boot toe. It rolled slightly out of its blue and white cloth, screwed its hideous little green face up even more, and continued wailing.

Though he had already downed the contents of one bottle of mead and was well into the second, Blackmoore's mind was still sharp. Now, an idea began to form in his head. Ignoring Tammis's unhappy warnings, Blackmoore bent over and picked up the small monster, tucking the blue and white cloth snugly about it. Almost immediately, it stopped crying. Blue-gray eyes locked with his.

"Interesting," said Blackmoore. "Their infants have blue eyes when they are young, just as humans do." Soon enough those eyes would turn piggy and black, or red, and gaze upon all humans with murderous hate.

Unless. . . .

For years, Blackmoore had worked twice as hard to be half as well regarded as other men of equal birth and rank. He had labored under the stigma of his father's treachery, and had done everything possible to gain power and position. He was still skeptically regarded by many; "blood of a traitor" was often muttered when those around him thought him unable to hear. But now, perhaps he might one day not have to listen to those cutting comments any longer.

"Tammis," he said thoughtfully, gazing intently into the incongruously soft blue of the baby orc's eyes, "did you know that you have the honor to serve a brilliant man?"

"Of course I did, sir," Tammis replied, as was expected. "May I inquire as to why this is particularly true at this moment?"

Blackmoore glanced up at the still-mounted servant, and grinned. "Because Lieutenant Aedelas Blackmoore holds in his hands something that is going to make him famous, wealthy, and best of all, powerful."

TWO

Tammis Foxton was in a state of high agitation, due directly and inevitably to the fact that his master was terribly displeased. When they had brought the orc whelp home Blackmoore had been much as he was on the battlefield: alert, interested, focused.

The orcs were proving less and less of a challenge each day, and men used to the excitement of almost daily battles were growing bored. The planned bouts were proving extremely popular, giving men an outlet for their pent-up energies and providing a chance for a little money to change hands as well.

And this orc was going to be raised firmly under human control. With the speed and power of the orcs, but the knowledge that Blackmoore would impart, he would be all but unconquerable in the planned matches that were beginning to spring up.

Except the ugly little thing wouldn't eat, and had grown pale and quiet over the last several days. Nobody said the words, but everyone knew. The beast was dying.

That had enraged Blackmoore. Once, he had even seized the small monster and tried to shove finely chopped meat down its throat. He succeeded only in nearly choking the orc, whom he had named "Thrall," and when Thrall had spat up the meat he had literally dropped the orc on the straw and strode, cursing, from the stable in which the orc was temporarily housed.

Now Tammis walked around his master with the utmost discretion, choosing his words even more carefully than usual. And yet, more often than not, he had left an encounter with Lieutenant Blackmoore with a bottle—sometimes empty, sometimes not—flying behind him.

His wife Clannia, a fair-haired, apple-cheeked woman who served in the kitchens, now set a plate of cold food in front of him on the wooden table and rubbed his tight neck as he sat down to eat. Compared to Blackmoore, the beefy, loud cook who ran the kitchens was a veritable Paladin.

"Any word?" Clannia asked hopefully. She awkwardly sat down beside him at the rough wooden table. She had given birth a few weeks ago and still moved with hesitation. She and their eldest daughter, Taretha, had eaten many hours ago. Unseen by either parent, the girl, who slept with her baby brother in a small bed beside the hearth, had woken at her father's entrance. Now she sat up, her yellow curls covered by a sleeping cap, and watched and listened to the adult conversation.

"Aye, and all bad," said Tammis heavily as he spooned congealing potato soup into his mouth. He chewed, swallowed, and continued. "The orc is dying. It won't take anything Blackmoore tries to feed it."

Clannia sighed and reached for her mending. The needle flashed back and forth, stitching together a new dress for Taretha. "It's only right," she said softly. "Blackmoore had no business bringing something like that into Durnholde. Bad enough we've got the mature ones screaming all day long. I can't wait until the internment camps are finished and they're no longer Durnholde's problem." She shuddered.

Taretha watched, silent. Her eyes were wide. She had heard vague mutterings about a baby orc, but this was the first chance she had had to hear her parents discussing it. Her young mind raced. Orcs were so big and scary-looking, with their sharp teeth, green skin, and deep voices. She'd only caught the barest glimpses of them, but she had heard all the stories. But a baby wouldn't be big and scary. She glanced over at the small figure of her brother. Even as she watched, Faralyn stirred, opened his rosebud mouth, and announced that he was hungry with a shrill cry.

In a smooth motion, Clannia rose, put down her sewing, picked up her son, bared a breast, and set him to nursing. "Taretha!" she scolded. "You should be asleep."

"I was," Taretha said, rising and running to her father. "I heard Da come in."

Tammis smiled tiredly and permitted Taretha to climb in his lap. "She won't go back to sleep until Faralyn is done," he told Clannia. "Let me hold her for a while. I so seldom get to see her, and she's growing like a weed." He pinched her cheek gently and she giggled.

"If the orc dies, it will go badly with all of us here," he continued.

Taretha frowned. The answer was obvious. "Da," she said, "if it's a baby, why are you trying to make it eat meat?"

Both adults stared at her, stunned. "What do you mean, little one?" asked Tammis in a strained voice.

Taretha pointed to her nursing brother. "Babies drink milk, like Faralyn does. If this baby orc's mother is dead, it can't drink its milk."

Tammis continued to stare; then a slow smile spread across his weary face. "Out of the mouths of babes," he whispered, and then hugged his daughter to him so tightly that she began to squirm in protest.

"Tammis. . . ." Clannia's voice was taut.

"My dearest," he said. He held Taretha with one arm and reached across the table to his wife with the other. "Tari's right. For all their barbaric ways, the orcs do nurse their young, as we do. Our best guess is that the orc infant is but a few months old. It's no wonder it

can't yet eat meat. It doesn't even have any teeth yet."
He hesitated, but Clannia's face grew pale, as if she
knew what he was going to say.

"You can't mean . . . you can't ask me to. . . ."

"Think what it will mean to our family!" Tammis exclaimed. "I've served Blackmoore for ten years. I've
never seen him this excited about anything. If that orc
survives because of us, we will lack for nothing!"

"I . . . I *can't,*" stammered Clannia.

"Can't what?" asked Taretha, but they both ignored her.

"Please," begged Tammis. "It's only for a little while."

"They're monsters, Tam!" cried Clannia. "Monsters,
and you . . . you want me to. . . ." She covered her face
with one hand and began to sob. The baby continued
to nurse, unperturbed.

"Da, why is Ma crying?" asked Taretha, anxious.

"I'm not crying," said Clannia thickly. She wiped her
wet face and forced a smile. "See, darling? All is well."
She looked at Tammis, and swallowed hard. "Your Da
just has something he needs me to do, that's all."

When Blackmoore heard that his personal servant's
wife had agreed to wet-nurse the dying orc baby, the
Foxton family was deluged with gifts. Rich fabrics, the
freshest fruits and choicest meats, fine beeswax ta-
pers—all began to appear regularly at the door of the
small room that the family called their home. Soon,
that room was exchanged for another, and then for

larger quarters still. Tammis Foxton was given his own horse, a lovely bay he named Ladyfire. Clannia, now called Mistress Foxton, no longer had to report to the kitchens, but spent all her time with her children and tending to the needs of what Blackmoore called his "special project." Taretha wore fine clothes and even had a tutor, a fussy, kind man named Jaramin Skisson, sent to teach her to read and write, like a lady.

But she was never allowed to speak about the small creature that lived with them for the next full year, who, when Faralyn died of a fever, became the only baby in the Foxton household. And when Thrall had learned to eat a vile concoction of blood, cow's milk, and porridge with his own small hands, three armed guards came and wrested him away from Taretha's arms. She cried and protested, and received a harsh blow for her pleas.

Her father held her and shushed her, kissing her pale cheek where a red hand imprint was visible. She quieted after a while, and, like the obedient child she wished to appear, agreed never to speak of Thrall again except in the most casual of terms.

But she vowed she would never forget this strange creature that had been almost like a younger brother to her.

Never.

"No, no. Like this." Jaramin Skisson stepped beside his pupil. "Hold it thus, with your fingers here . . . and here. Ah, that's better. Now make this motion . . . like a snake."

"What is a snake?" asked Thrall. He was only six years old, but already almost as big as his tutor. His large, clumsy hands did not hold the delicate, thin stylus easily, and the clay tablet kept slipping out of his grasp. But he was stubborn, and determined to master this letter that Jaramin called an "S."

Jaramin blinked behind his large spectacles. "Oh, of course," he said, more to himself than Thrall. "A snake is a reptile with no feet. It looks like this letter."

Thrall brightened with recognition. "Like a worm," he said. He had often snacked on those small treats that found their way into his cell.

"Yes, it does resemble a worm. Try it again, on your own this time." Thrall stuck his tongue out to aid his concentration. A shaky form appeared on the clay, but he knew it was recognizable as an "S." Proud of himself, he extended it to Jaramin.

"Very good, Thrall! I think it may be time we started teaching you numbers," said the tutor.

"But first, it's time to start learning how to fight, eh, Thrall?" Thrall looked up to see the lean form of his master, Lieutenant Blackmoore, standing in the doorway. He stepped inside. Thrall heard the lock click shut on the other side of the door. He had never tried to flee, but the guards always seemed to expect him to.

At once Thrall prostrated himself as Blackmoore

had taught him. A kindly pat on his head told him he had permission to rise. He stumbled to his feet, suddenly feeling even bigger and clumsier than usual. He looked down at Blackmoore's boots, awaiting whatever it was his master had in store for him.

"How is he coming in his lessons?" Blackmoore asked Jaramin, as if Thrall weren't present.

"Very well. I hadn't realized orcs were quite so intelligent, but—"

"He is intelligent not because he is an orc," Blackmoore interrupted, his voice sharp enough to make Thrall flinch. "He is intelligent because humans taught him. Never forget that, Jaramin. And you." The boots turned in Thrall's direction. "You aren't to forget that either."

Thrall shook his head violently.

"Look at me, Thrall."

Thrall hesitated, then lifted his blue-eyed gaze. Blackmoore's eyes bored into his own. "Do you know what your name means?"

"No, sir." His voice sounded so rough and deep, even in his own ears, next to the musical lilt of the humans' voices.

"It means 'slave.' It means that you belong to me." Blackmoore stepped forward and prodded the orc's chest with a stiff forefinger. "It means that I *own you*. Do you understand that?"

For a moment, Thrall was so shocked he didn't reply. His name meant *slave*? It sounded so pleasant when humans spoke it, he thought it must be a good name, a worthy name.

Blackmoore's gloved hand came up and slapped Thrall across the face. Although the lieutenant had swung his hand with vigor, Thrall's skin was so thick and tough that the orc barely felt it. And yet the blow pained him deeply. His master had struck him! One large hand came up to touch the cheek, its black fingernails clipped short.

"You answer when you're spoken to," snapped Blackmoore. "Do you understand what I just said?"

"Yes, Master Blackmoore," replied Thrall, his deep voice barely a whisper.

"Excellent." Blackmoore's angry face relaxed into an approving smile. His teeth showed white against the surrounding black hair of his goatee. That quickly, all was well again. Relief surged through Thrall. His lips turned up in his best approximation of Blackmoore's smile.

"Don't do that, Thrall," said Blackmoore. "It makes you look uglier than you already are."

Abruptly, the smile vanished.

"Lieutenant," said Jaramin softly, "he's just trying to mimic your smile, that's all."

"Well, he shouldn't. Humans smile. Orcs don't. You said he was doing well in his lessons, yes? Can he read and write, then?"

"He is reading at quite an advanced level. As for writing, he understands how, but those thick fingers are having a difficult time with some of the lettering."

"Excellent," Blackmoore said again. "Then we have no more need of your services."

Thrall inhaled swiftly and looked over at Jaramin. The older man appeared to be as surprised as he by the statement.

"There's much he doesn't know yet, sir," stammered Jaramin. "He knows little of numbers, of history, of art—"

"He doesn't need to master history, and I can teach him what he needs to know about numbers myself. And what does a slave need to know of art, hmm? I fancy you think that would be a waste of time, eh, Thrall?"

Thrall thought briefly of the one time Jaramin had brought in a small statue and told him how it was carved, of how they had discussed how his swaddling cloth with its once-bright colors of blue and white had been woven. That, Jaramin had said, was "art," and Thrall had been eager to learn more about making such beautiful things.

"As my master wishes, so does Thrall," he said obediently, giving the lie to the feelings in his heart.

"That's right. You don't need to know those things, Thrall. You need to learn how to fight." With uncharacteristic affection, Blackmoore reached out a hand and placed it on Thrall's enormous shoulder. Thrall flinched, then stared at his master.

"I wanted you to learn reading and writing because it might one day give you an advantage over your opponent. I'm going to see to it that you are skilled with every weapon I have ever seen. I'm going to teach you about strategy, Thrall, and trickery. You are going to be famous in the gladiator ring. Thousands will chant your name when you appear. How does that sound, eh?"

Thrall saw Jaramin turn and gather up his things. It pained him strangely to see the stylus and the clay tablet disappear for the last time into Jaramin's sack. With a quick, backward glance, Jaramin moved to the door and knocked on it. It opened for him. He slipped out, and the door was closed and locked.

Blackmoore was waiting for Thrall's response. Thrall was a fast learner, and did not wish to be struck again for hesitating in his answer. Forcing himself to sound as if he believed it, he told his master, "That sounds exciting. I am glad my master wishes me to follow this path."

For the first time he could remember, Thrall the orc stepped out of his cell. He gazed in wonder as, with two guards in front of him, two guards behind, and Blackmoore keeping pace, he went through several winding stone corridors. They went up a set of stairs, then across, then down a winding stair that was so small it seemed to press in on Thrall.

Ahead was a brightness that made Thrall blink. They were approaching that brightness, and the fear of the unknown set in. When the guards ahead of him went through and into this area, Thrall froze. The ground ahead was yellow and brown, not the familiar gray of stone. Black things that resembled the guards lay on the ground, following their every movement.

"What are you doing?" snapped Blackmoore. "Come out. Others held here would give their right arms to be able to walk out into the sunlight."

Thrall knew the word. "Sunlight" was what came through in small slats in his cell. But there was so much sunlight out there! And what of the strange black things? What were they?

Thrall pointed at the black human-shaped things on the ground. To his shame, all the guards started laughing. One of them was soon wiping tears of mirth from his face. Blackmoore turned red.

"You idiot," he said, "those are just—By the Light, have I gotten myself an orc who's afraid of his own shadow?" He gestured and one of the guards pricked Thrall's back deeply with the point of a spear. Although his naturally thick skin protected him, the prod stung and Thrall lurched forward.

His eyes burned, and he lifted his hands to cover them. And yet the sudden warmth of the . . . sunlight . . . on his head and back felt good. Slowly he lowered his hands and blinked, letting his eyes become accustomed to the light.

Something huge and green loomed in front of him.

Instinctively, he drew himself up to his full height and roared at it. More laughter from the guards, but this time, Blackmoore nodded in approval at Thrall's reaction.

"That's a mock fighter," he said. "It's only made of burlap and stuffing and paint, Thrall. It's a troll."

Again embarrassment flamed through Thrall. Now

that he looked more closely, he could tell it was no living thing. Straw served the mock fighter for hair, and he could see where it was stitched together.

"Does a troll really look like that?" he asked.

Blackmoore chuckled. "Only vaguely," said Blackmoore. "It wasn't designed for realism, but for practice. Watch."

He extended a gloved arm and one of the guards handed him something. "This is a wooden sword," Blackmoore explained. "A sword is a weapon, and we use wood for practice. Once you're sufficiently trained with this, you'll move on to the real thing."

Blackmoore held the sword in both hands. He centered himself, then raced at the practice troll. He managed to strike it three times, once in the head, once in the body, and once along the false arm that held a cloth weapon, without breaking stride. Breathing only slightly heavily, he turned around and trotted back. "Now you try," he said.

Thrall held out his hand for the weapon. His thick fingers closed around it. It fit his palm much better than the stylus had. It felt better, too, almost familiar. He adjusted the grip, trying to do what he had seen Blackmoore do.

"Very good," said Blackmoore. To one of the guards, he said, "Look at that, will you? He's a natural. As I knew he would be. Now, Thrall . . . attack!"

Thrall whirled. For the first time in his life, his body seemed willing to do what he asked of it. He lifted the sword, and to his surprise, a roar burst forth from his throat. His legs began to pump almost of their own accord, smoothly and swiftly carrying him toward the mock troll. He lifted the sword—oh, it was so easy—and brought it down in a smooth arc across the troll's body.

There was a terrible crack and the troll went sailing through the air. Suddenly afraid he had done something terribly wrong, Thrall's grace turned to clumsiness and he stumbled over his own feet. He hit the earth hard and felt the wooden sword crack underneath him.

Thrall scrambled to his feet and prostrated himself, sure that some sort of terrible punishment was about to ensue. He had broken the mock troll and destroyed the practice sword. He was so big, so clumsy . . . !

Loud whoops filled the air. Other than Jaramin, the silent guards, and the occasional visit from Blackmoore, Thrall had not had much interaction with humans. Certainly he had not learned to discern the finer points in their wordless noises, but he had a strange suspicion that these were not sounds of anger. Cautiously he looked up.

Blackmoore had an enormous smile on his face, as did the guards. One of them was bringing the palms of his hands together to create a loud smacking sound. When he caught sight of Thrall, Blackmoore's smile widened even more.

"Did I not say he would surpass all expectations?" cried Blackmoore. "Well done, Thrall! Well done!"

Thrall blinked, uncertain. "I . . . that wasn't wrong?" he asked. "The troll and the sword . . . I broke them."

"Damn right you did! First time ever swinging a sword and the troll sails across the courtyard!" Blackmoore's giddiness subsided slightly and he put his arm around the young orc in a friendly manner. Thrall tensed, then relaxed.

"Suppose you were in the gladiator ring," Blackmoore said. "Suppose that troll was real, that your sword was real. And suppose the first time you charged, you struck him so hard that he fell that far. Don't you see that that's a good thing, Thrall?"

The orc supposed he did. His large lips wanted to stretch over his teeth in a smile, but he resisted the impulse. Blackmoore had never been so pleased with him, so kind to him, before, and he wished to do nothing to disturb the moment.

Blackmoore squeezed Thrall's shoulder, then returned to his men. "You!" he shouted to a guard. "Get that troll back on the pike, and make sure it's secure enough to withstand my Thrall's mighty blows. You, get me another practice sword. Hells, get me five of them. Thrall is liable to break them all!"

Out of the corner of his eye, Thrall saw movement. He turned to see a tall, slender man with curly hair dressed in livery red, black, and gold that marked him as one of Blackmoore's servants. With him was a very small human being with bright yellow hair. It looked nothing like the guards that Thrall knew. He wondered if this was a human child. It looked softer, and its garments were not the trousers and tunics the other wore, but a long, flowing garment that brushed the dusty earth. Was this, then, a female child?

His eyes locked with the blue ones of the child. She did not seem frightened of his ugly appearance at all. On the contrary, she met his gaze evenly, and as he watched, she smiled brightly and waved at him, as if she was happy to see him.

How could such a thing be? Even as Thrall watched, trying to determine the proper response, the male accompanying her clamped a hand to the little female's shoulder and steered her away.

Wondering what had just happened, Thrall turned back to the cheering men, and closed his large, green hand about another practice sword.

THREE

A routine was quickly established, one that Thrall would follow for the next several years. He would be fed at dawn, his hands and feet clapped in manacles that permitted him to shuffle out to the courtyard of Durnholde, and there he would train. At first, Blackmoore himself conducted the training, showing him the basic mechanics and often praising him effusively. Sometimes, though, Blackmoore's temper was sharp and nothing Thrall could do would please him. At such times, the nobleman's speech was slightly slurred, his movements haphazard, and he would berate the orc for no reason that Thrall could discern. Thrall came to simply accept the fact that he was unworthy. If Blackmoore berated him, it must be because he deserved it; any praise was simply the lord's own kindness.

After a few months, though, another man stepped in

and Thrall ceased to see Blackmoore regularly. This man, known to Thrall only as Sergeant, was huge by human standards. He stood well over six feet, with a thick barrel chest covered with curly red hair. The hair on his head was bright red, its tousled mop matched by the long beard. He wore a black scarf knotted around his throat and in one ear sported a large earring. The first day he came to address Thrall and the other fighters who were being trained alongside him, he had fixed each one with a hard stare and shouted out the challenge.

"See this?" He pointed with a stubby forefinger to the glistening hoop in his left ear. "I haven't taken this out in thirteen years. I've trained thousands of recruits just like you pups. And with each group I offer the same challenge: Rip this earring from my ear and I'll let you beat me to a pulp." He grinned, showing several missing teeth. "You don't think it now, p'raps, but by the time I'm done with you, you'd sell your own mother for the chance to take a swing at me. But if I'm ever so slow that I can't fend off an attack by any of you ladies, then I deserve to have my ear ripped off and be forced to swallow what's left of my teeth."

He had been walking slowly down the line of men and now stopped abruptly in front of Thrall. "That goes double for you, you overgrown goblin," Sergeant snarled.

Thrall lowered his gaze, confused. He had been taught never, ever, to raise his hand against humans.

And yet it appeared as though he was to fight them. There was no way he would ever try to rip Sergeant's earring from his lobe.

A large hand slipped underneath Thrall's chin and jerked it up. "You look at me when I talk to you, you understand?"

Thrall nodded, now hopelessly confused. Blackmoore didn't want him to meet his gaze. This man had just ordered him to do exactly that. What was he to do?

Sergeant divided them into pairs. The number was uneven and Thrall stood alone. Sergeant marched right up to him and tossed a wooden sword to him. Instinctively, Thrall caught it. Sergeant grunted in approval.

"Good eye-hand coordination," he said. Like all the other men, he carried a shield and was wearing heavy, well-cushioned armor that would protect his body and head. Thrall had none. His skin was so thick that he barely felt the blows as it was, and he was growing so quickly that any clothing or armor fashioned for him would soon be far too small.

"Let's see how you defend yourself, then!" And with no further warning, Sergeant charged Thrall.

For the briefest second, Thrall shrank from the attack. Then something inside him seemed to click into place. He no longer moved from a place of fear and confusion, but a place of confidence. He stood up straight, to his full height, and realized that he was growing so quickly that he was taller even than his opponent. He lifted his left arm, which he knew would one day hold a shield heavier than a human, in defense against the wooden sword, and brought his own practice weapon down in a smooth arc. If Sergeant had not reacted with stunning speed, Thrall's sword would have slammed into his helm. And even with that protection, Thrall knew that the power behind his blow was such that Sergeant probably would have been killed.

But Sergeant was swift, and his shield blocked Thrall's likely fatal blow. Thrall grunted in surprise as Sergeant landed a blow of his own against Thrall's bare midsection. He stumbled, thrown briefly off balance.

Sergeant took the opening and pressed, landing three swift blows that would have killed an unarmored man. Thrall regained his footing and felt a strange, hot emotion surge through him. Suddenly, his world narrowed to the figure before him. All his frustration and helplessness fled, replaced by a deadly focus: *Kill Sergeant.*

He screamed aloud, the power of his own voice startling even him, then charged. He lifted his weapon and struck, lifted and struck, raining blows upon the big man. Sergeant tried to retreat and his booted feet slipped on a stone. He fell backward. Thrall cried out again, as a keen desire to smash Sergeant's head to a pulp swept through him like a white-hot tide. Sergeant managed to get the sword in front of him and deflected most of the blows, but now Thrall had him pinned between his powerful legs. He tossed aside his sword and reached out with his large hands. If he could just fasten them around Blackmoore's neck—

Appalled at the image that swam before his eyes, Thrall froze, his fingers inches away from Sergeant's throat. It was protected with a gorget, of course, but Thrall's fingers were powerful. If he had managed to clamp down—

And then several men were on him all at once, shouting at him and hauling him off the prone figure of the fighting instructor. Now it was Thrall who was on his back, his mighty arms lifted to ward off the blows of several swords. He heard a strange sound, a *clang,* and then saw something metallic catch the bright sunlight.

"Hold!" screamed Sergeant, his voice as loud and commanding as if he had not just been inches away from death. "Damn you, hold or I'll cut your bloody arm off! Sheathe your sword this minute, Maridan!"

Thrall heard a *snick.* Then two strong arms seized his and he was hauled to his feet. He stared at Sergeant.

To his utter surprise, Sergeant laughed out loud and clapped a hand on the orc's shoulder. "Good job, lad. That's the closest I've ever come to having me earring snatched—and in the first match at that. You're a born warrior, but you forgot the goal, didn't you?" He pointed to the gold hoop. "This was the goal, not squeezing the life out of me."

Thrall struggled to speak. "I am sorry, Sergeant. I don't know what happened. You attacked, and then. . . ." He was not about to tell of the brief image of Blackmoore he had had. It was bad enough that he had lost his head.

"Some foes, you're going to want to do what you just did," said Sergeant, surprising him. "Good tactics there. But some opponents, like all the humans you'll face, you're going to want to get 'em down and then end it. Stop there. The bloodlust might save your hide in a real battle, but for gladiator fighting, you'll need to be more here—" he tapped the side of his head "—than here," and he patted his gut. "I want you to read some books on strategy. You read, don't you?"

"A little," Thrall managed.

"You need to learn the history of battle campaigns. These pups all know it," and he waved at the other young soldiers. "For a time, that will be their advantage." He turned to glare at them. "But only for a time, lads. This one's got courage and strength, and he's but a babe yet."

The men shot Thrall hostile glances. Thrall felt a sudden warmth, a happiness he had never known. He had nearly killed this man, but had not been reprimanded. Instead, he had been told he needed to learn, to improve, to know when to go for the kill and when to show . . . what? What did one call it when one spared an opponent?

"Sergeant," he asked, wondering if he would be punished for even voicing the question, "sometimes . . . you said sometimes you don't kill. Why not?"

Sergeant regarded him evenly. "It's called mercy, Thrall," he said quietly. "And you'll learn about that, too."

Mercy. Under his breath, Thrall turned the word over on his tongue. It was a sweet word.

"You let him do that to you?" Though Tammis was not supposed to be privy to this particular conversation between his master and the man he had hired to train Thrall, Blackmoore's shrill voice carried. Pausing in his duty of cleaning the mud off of Blackmoore's boots, Tammis strained to listen. He did not think of this as eavesdropping. He thought of this as a vital way to protect his family's welfare.

"It was a good martial move." Sergeant Something-or-other replied, sounding not at all defensive. "I treated it the way I would had it been any other man."

"But Thrall isn't a man, he's an orc! Or hadn't you noticed?"

"Aye, I had," said Sergeant. Tammis maneuvered himself so that he could peer through the half-closed door. Sergeant looked out of place in Blackmoore's richly decorated receiving room. "And it's not my place to ask why you want 'im trained so thorough."

"You're right about that."

"But you *do* want 'im trained thorough," said Sergeant. "And that's exactly what I'm doing."

"By letting him nearly kill you?"

"By praising a good move, and teaching 'im when it's good to use the bloodlust and when it's good to keep a cool head!" growled Sergeant. Tammis smothered a smile. Evidently, it was becoming difficult for

Sergeant to keep his. "But that's not the reason I've come. I understand you taught 'im to read. I want 'im to have a look at some books."

Tammis gaped.

"What?" cried Blackmoore.

Tammis had utterly forgotten the chore he was ostensibly performing. He stared through the crack in the door, a brush in one hand and a muddy boot in the other, listening intently. When there was a light tap at his shoulder, he nearly jumped out of his skin.

Heart thudding, he whirled to behold Taretha. She grinned impishly at him, her blue eyes flicking from those of her father to the door. Clearly, she knew exactly what he was doing.

Tammis was embarrassed. But that emotion was overridden by a passionate desire to know what was about to happen. He raised a finger to his lips and Taretha nodded wisely.

"Now, why did you go and teach an orc to read if you didn't want him doing so?"

Blackmoore spluttered something incoherent.

" 'E's got a brain, whatever else you may think of him, and if you wants 'im trained the way you told me, you've got to get him understanding battle tactics, maps, strategies, siege techniques—"

Sergeant was calmly ticking things off on his fingers. "All right!" Blackmoore exploded. "Though I imagine I'll live to regret this. . . ." He strode toward the wall of books and quickly selected a few. "Taretha!" he bellowed.

Both older and younger Foxton servants jumped. Quickly Taretha smoothed her hair, put on a pleasant expression, and entered the room.

She dropped a curtsy. "Yes, sir?"

"Here." Blackmoore thrust the books at her. They were large and cumbersome and filled her arms. She peered at him over the edge of the top book, only her eyes visible. "I want you to give these to Thrall's guard to give him."

"Yes, sir," Taretha replied, as if this were something she was asked to do every day and not one of the most shocking things Tammis had heard his master order. "They're a bit heavy, sir . . . may I go to my quarters for a sack? It will make the carrying easier."

She looked every inch the obedient little servant girl. Only Tammis and Clannia knew how sharp a brain—and tongue—were hidden behind that deceptively sweet visage. Blackmoore softened slightly and patted her fair head.

"Of course, child. But take them straight over, understood?"

"Indeed, sir. Thank you, sir." She seemed to try to curtsy, thought better of it, and left.

Tammis closed the door behind her. Taretha turned to him, her large eyes shining. "Oh, Da!" she breathed, her voice soft so it would not carry. "I'm going to get to see him!"

Tammis's heart sank. He had hoped she was over this disturbing interest in the orc's welfare. "No,

Taretha. You're just to hand the books to the guards, is all."

Her face fell, and she turned away sadly. "It's just . . . since Faralyn died . . . he's the only little brother I have."

"He's not your brother, he's an orc. An animal, fit only for camps or gladiator battles. Remember that." Tammis hated disappointing his daughter in anything, but it was for the child's own good. She mustn't be noticed having an interest in Thrall. Only ill would come from that if Blackmoore ever found out.

Thrall was sound asleep, worn out from the excitement of the day's practice, when the door to his cell slammed open. He blinked sleepily, then got to his feet as one of the guards entered carrying a large sack.

"Lieutenant says these are for you. He wants you to finish them all and be able to talk with him about them," said the guard. There was a hint of contempt in his voice, but Thrall thought nothing of it. The guards always spoke to him with contempt.

The door was pulled closed and locked. Thrall looked at the sack. With a delicacy that belied his huge frame, he untied the knot and reached inside. His fingers closed on something rectangular and firm, but that gave slightly.

It couldn't be. He remembered the feel. . . .

Hardly daring to hope, he pulled it forth into the dim light of his cell and stared at it. It was, indeed, a book. He read the title, sounding it aloud: *"The History of the Alliance of Lor-lordaeron."* Eagerly he grabbed a second book, and a third. They were all military history books. As he flipped one open, something fluttered to the straw-covered floor of his cell. It was a small, tightly folded piece of parchment.

Curious, he unfolded it, taking his time with his large fingers. It was a note. His lips worked, but he did not speak aloud:

Dear Thrall,

Master B. has ordered that you have these books I am so excited for you. I did not know he had let you learn how to read. He let me learn how to read too and I love reading. I miss you and hope you are well. It looks like what they are making you do in the courtyard hurts I hope you are all right. I would like to keep talking with you do you want to? If yes, write me a note on the back of this paper and fold it back up in the book I put it in. I will try to come and see you if not keep looking for me Im the little girl who waved at you that one time. I hope you write back!!!!!

Love Taretha

P.S. Dont tell anyone about the note we will get in BIG TROUBLE!!!

Thrall sat down heavily. He could not believe what he had just read. He remembered the small female child, and had wondered why she had waved at him. Clearly, she knew him and . . . and thought *well* of him. How could this be? Who was she?

He extended a forefinger and gazed at the blunted, clipped nail. It would have to do. On his left arm, a scratch was healing. Thrall jabbed as deeply as he could and after several tries managed to tear the small wound open again. A sluggish trickle of crimson rewarded his efforts. Using his nail as a stylus, he carefully wrote on the back of the note a single word:

YES.

FOUR

Thrall was twelve years old when he saw his first orc.

He was training outside the fortress grounds. Once he had won his first battle at the tender age of eight, Blackmoore had agreed with Sergeant's plan to give the orc more freedom—at least in training. He still had a manacle fastened to one of his feet, which was in turn carefully attached to a huge boulder. Not even an orc of Thrall's strength would be able to flee with that attached to his leg. The chains were thick and sturdy, unlikely to break. After the first time or two, Thrall paid it no heed. The chain was long and gave him plenty of room to maneuver. The thought of escaping had never occurred to him. He was Thrall, the slave. Blackmoore was his master, Sergeant his trainer, Taretha his secret friend. All was as it should be.

Thrall regretted that he had never made friends with any of the men with whom he practiced. Each year there was a new group, and they were all cut of the same cloth: young, eager, contemptuous, and slightly frightened of the mammoth green being with whom they were expected to train. Only Sergeant ever gave him a compliment; only Sergeant interfered when one or more would gang up on Thrall. At times Thrall wished he could fight back, but he remembered the concept of honorable fighting. Although these men thought of him as the enemy, he knew they weren't, and killing or grievously wounding them was the wrong thing to do.

Thrall had sharp ears and always paid attention to the idle gossip of the men. Because they thought him a mindless brute, they were not too careful of their tongues in his presence. Who minds their words when the only witness is an animal? It was in this way that Thrall learned that the orcs, once a fearful enemy, were weakening. More and more of them were being caught and rounded up into something called "internment camps." Durnholde was the base, and all those in charge of these camps lodged here now, while underlings conducted the day-to-day running of the camps. Blackmoore was the head of all of them. There were a few skirmishes still, but less and less frequently. Some of the men present at the training had never seen an orc fighting before they encountered Thrall.

Over the years, Sergeant had taught Thrall the finer

points of hand-to-hand combat. Thrall was versed in every weapon used in the fights: sword, broadsword, spear, morningstar, dagger, scourge, net, ax, club, and halberd. He had been granted the barest of armor; it was deemed more exciting for the watching crowds if the combatants had little protection.

Now he stood at the center of a group of trainees. This was familiar territory to him, and was more for the benefit of the young men than for him. Sergeant called this scenario "ringing." The trainees were (of course) humans who had supposedly come upon one of the few remaining renegade orcs, who was determined not to go down without a fight. Thrall was (of course) the defiant orc. The idea was for them to devise at least three different ways of capturing or killing the "rogue orc."

Thrall was not particularly fond of this scenario. He much preferred one-on-one fighting to being the target of sometimes as many as twelve men. The light in the men's eyes at the thought of fighting him, and the smiles on their lips, always dismayed Thrall. The first time Sergeant had enacted the scenario, Thrall had had difficulty in summoning up the necessary resistance required in order to make this an effective teaching tool. Sergeant had to take him aside and assure him it was all right to pretend. The men had armor and real weapons; he had only a wooden practice sword. It was unlikely Thrall would cause any lasting harm.

So now, after having performed this routine several times over the last few years, Thrall immediately became a snarling, ravening beast. The first few times, it had been difficult to separate fantasy from reality, but it became easier with practice. He would never lose control in this scenario, and if things did turn bad, he trusted Sergeant with his life.

Now they advanced on him. Predictably, they chose simple assault as their first of three tactics. Two had swords, four had spears, and the rest had axes. One of them lunged.

Thrall swiftly parried, his wooden sword flying up with startling speed. He lifted a massive leg and kicked out, striking the attacker full in the chest. The young man went hurtling backward, astonishment plain on his face. He lay on the ground, gasping for air.

Thrall whirled, anticipating the approach of two others. They came at him with spears. With the sword, he knocked one of them out of the way as easily as if the human had been an annoying insect. With his free hand, for he had no shield, he seized the other man's spear, yanked it from his grip, and flipped it around so that the sharp blade was facing the man who had, just seconds ago, been wielding the weapon.

Had this been a real battle, Thrall knew he would have sunk the spear into the man's body. But this was just practice, and Thrall was in control. He lifted the spear and was about to toss it away when a terrible sound made everyone freeze in his tracks.

Thrall turned to see a small wagon approaching the fortress on the small, winding road. This happened many times each day, and the passengers were always the same: farmers, merchants, new recruits, visiting dignitaries of some sort.

Not this time.

This time, the screaming horses pulled a wagon full of monstrous green creatures. They were in a metal cage, and seemed stooped over. Thrall saw that they were chained to the bottom of the wagon. He was filled with horror at their grotesqueness. They were huge, deformed, sported mammoth tusks instead of teeth, had tiny, fierce eyes. . . .

And then the truth hit him. These were orcs. His so-called people. This was what he looked like to the humans. The practice sword fell from suddenly nerveless fingers. *I'm hideous. I'm frightening. I'm a monster. No wonder they hate me so.*

One of the beasts turned and stared Thrall right in the eye. He wanted to look away, but couldn't. He stared back, hardly breathing. Even as he watched, the orc somehow managed to wrench himself free. With a scream that shattered Thrall's ears, the creature hurled himself at the cage bars. He reached with hands bloody from the chafing of shackles, gripped the bars, and before Thrall's shocked eyes bent them wide enough to push his huge bulk through. The wagon was still moving as the frightened horses ran at top speed. The orc hit the ground hard and rolled a few times, but a heart-beat later was up and running toward Thrall and the fighters with a speed that belied his size.

He opened his terrible mouth and screamed out something that sounded like words: "Kagh! Bin mog g'thazag cha!"

"Attack, you fools!" cried Sergeant. Unarmored as he was, he seized a sword and began running to meet the orc. The men began to move and rushed to their Sergeant's aid.

The orc didn't even bother to look Sergeant in the face. He swung out with his manacled left hand, caught Sergeant square in the chest, and sent him flying. He came on, implacable. His eyes were fastened on Thrall, and again he shouted the words, "Kagh! Bin mog g'thazag cha!"

Thrall stirred, finally roused from his fear, but he didn't know what to do. He raised his practice sword and stood in a defensive posture, but did not advance. This fearfully ugly thing was charging toward him. It was most definitely the enemy. And yet, it was one of his own people, his flesh and blood. An orc, just as Thrall was an orc, and Thrall could not bring himself to attack.

Even as Thrall stared, the men fell upon the orc and the big green body went down beneath the flash of swords and axes and black armor. Blood seeped out beneath the pile of men, and when at last it was over, they stood back and regarded a pile of green and red flesh where a living creature had once been.

Sergeant propped himself up on one elbow. "Thrall!" he cried. "Get him back to the cell *now!*"

* * *

"What in the name of all that's holy have you *done*?" cried Blackmoore, staring aghast at the sergeant who had come to him so highly recommended, who was now the person Blackmoore had come to hate more than any other. "He was never supposed to see another orc, not until . . . now he knows, damn it. What were you thinking?"

Sergeant bristled under the verbal attack. "I was *thinking*, sir, that if you didn't want Thrall to see any other orcs, you might have told me that. I was *thinking*, sir, that if you didn't want Thrall to see other orcs you might have arranged for the wagons carrying them to approach when Thrall was in his cell. I was *thinking, sir,* that—"

"Enough!" bellowed Blackmoore. He took a deep breath and collected himself. "The damage is done. We must think how to repair it."

His calmer tone seemed to ease Sergeant as well. In a less belligerent tone, the trainer asked, "Thrall has never known what he looked like, then?"

"Never. No mirrors. No still basins of water. He's been taught that orcs are scum, which is of course true, and that he is permitted to live only because he earns me money."

Silence fell as the two men searched their thoughts. Sergeant scratched his red beard pensively, then said, "So he knows. So what? Just because he was born an orc doesn't mean he can't be more than that. He doesn't have to be a brainless brute. He isn't, in fact. If you encouraged him to think of himself as more human—"

Sergeant's suggestion infuriated Blackmoore. "He's not!" he burst out. "He *is* a brute. I don't want him getting ideas that he's nothing less than a big green-skinned human!"

"Then, pray, sir," said Sergeant, grinding out the words between clenched teeth, "what *do* you want him to think of himself as?"

Blackmoore had no response. He didn't know. He hadn't thought about it that way. It had seemed so simple when he had stumbled onto the infant orc. Raise him as a slave, train him to fight, give him the human edge, then put him in charge of an army of beaten orcs and attack the Alliance. With Thrall at the head of a revitalized orcish army, leading the charges, Blackmoore would have power beyond his most exaggerated fantasies.

But it wasn't working out that way. Deep inside, he knew that in some ways Sergeant was right. Thrall did need to understand how humans thought and reasoned if he was to take that knowledge to lord over the bestial orcs. And yet, if he learned, mightn't he revolt? Thrall had to be kept in his place, reminded of his low birth. *Had* to. By the Light, what was the right thing to do? How best to treat this creature in order to produce the perfect war leader, without letting anyone else know he was more than a gladiator champion?

He took a deep breath. He mustn't lose face in front of this servant. "Thrall needs direction, and we must give it to him," he said with remarkable calmness. "He's learned enough training with the recruits. I think it's time we relegated him exclusively to combat."

"Sir, he's very helpful in training," began Sergeant.

"We have all but vanquished the orcs," said Blackmoore, thinking of the thousands of orcs being shoved into the camps. "Their leader Doomhammer has fled, and they are a scattered race. Peace is descending upon us. We do not need to train the recruits to battle orcs any longer. Any battles in which they will participate will be against other men, not monsters."

Damn. He had almost said too much. Sergeant looked as if he had caught the slip, too, but did not react.

"Men at peace need an outlet for their bloodlust," he said. "Let us confine Thrall to the gladiator battles. He will fill our pockets and bring us honor." He smirked. "I've yet to see the single man who could stand up to an orc."

Thrall's ascendance in the ranks of the gladiators had been nothing short of phenomenal. He had reached his full height when very young; as the years passed, he began to add bulk to his tall frame. Now he was the biggest orc many had ever seen, even heard tell of. He was the master of the ring, and everyone knew it.

When he was not fighting he was shut alone in his cell, which seemed to him to grow smaller with each passing day despite the fact that Blackmoore had ordered him a new one. Thrall now had a small, covered sleeping area and a much larger area in which to practice. Covered by a grate, this sunken ring had mock weapons of every sort and Thrall's old friend, the battered training troll, upon which he could practice. Some nights, when he could not sleep, Thrall rose and took out his tension on the dummy.

It was the books that Taretha sent him, with their precious messages and now a tablet and stylus, that truly brightened those long, solitary hours. They had been conversing in secret at least once a week, and Thrall imagined a world as Tari painted it: A world of art, and beauty, and companionship. A world of food beyond rotting meat and slop. A world in which he had a place.

Every now and then, his eye would fall upon the increasingly fraying square of cloth that bore the symbol of a white wolf head on a blue field. He would look quickly away, not wanting to let his mind travel down that path. What good would it do? He had read enough books (some of which Blackmoore had no idea that Tari had passed along to Thrall) to understand that the orc people lived in small groups, each with its own distinctive symbol. What could he do, simply tell Blackmoore that he was tired of being a slave, thank you, and would he please let Thrall out so he could find his family?

And yet the thought teased him. His own people. Tari had her own people, her family of Tammis and Clannia Foxton. She was valued and loved. He was grateful that she had such loving support, because it was out of that secure place that she had felt large in heart enough to reach out to him.

Sometimes, he wondered what the rest of the Foxtons thought of him. Tari never mentioned them much anymore. She had told him that her mother Clannia had nursed him at her own breast, to save his life. At first, Thrall had been touched by that, but as he grew older and learned more, he understood that Clannia had not been moved to suckle him out of love, but out of a desire to increase her standing with Blackmoore.

Blackmoore. All roads of thought ended there. He could forget he was a piece of property when he was writing to Tari and reading her letters, or searching for her golden hair in the stands at the gladiator matches. He could also lose himself in the exciting thing Sergeant called "bloodlust." But these moments were all too brief. Even when Blackmoore himself came to visit Thrall, to discuss some military strategy Thrall had studied, or to play a game of Hawks and Hares with him, there was no link, no sense of family with this man. When Blackmoore was jovial, it was with the attitude of a man toward a child. And when he was irritable and darkly furious, which was more often than not, Thrall felt as helpless as a child. Blackmoore could order him beaten, or starved, or burned, or shackled, or—the worst punishment of all, and one that had, thankfully, not yet occurred to Blackmoore—deny him access to his books.

He knew that Tari did not have a privileged life, not the way Blackmoore did. She was a servant, in her own way, as much in thrall as the orc who bore the name. But she had friends, and she was not spat upon, and she *belonged*.

Slowly, his hand moved, of its own accord, to reach for the blue swaddling cloth. At that moment, he heard the door unlock and open behind him. He dropped the cloth as if it were something unclean.

"Come on," said one of the dour-faced guards. He extended the manacles. "Time to go fight. I hear they've got quite the opponents for you today." He grinned mirthlessly, showing brown teeth. "And Master Blackmoore's ready to have your hide if you don't win."

FIVE

Oore than a decade had passed since one Lieutenant Blackmoore had simultaneously found an orphaned orc and the possible answer to his dreams.

They had been fruitful and happy years for Thrall's master, and for humanity in general. Aedelas Blackmoore, once Lieutenant, now Lieutenant *General*, had been mocked about his "pet orc" when he had first brought it to Durnholde, especially when it seemed as though the wretched little thing wouldn't even survive. Thank goodness for Mistress Foxton and her swollen teats. Blackmoore couldn't conceive of any human female being willing to suckle an orc, but although the offer had increased his contempt for his servant and his family, it had also saved Blackmoore's behind. Which was why he hadn't begrudged them baubles, food, and education for their child, even if she was a girl.

It was a bright day, warm but not too hot. Perfect fighting weather. The awning, bright with his colors of red and gold, provided pleasant shade. Banners of all colors danced in the gentle breeze, and music and laughter floated to his ears. The smell of ripe fruits, fresh bread, and roasted venison teased his nostrils. Everyone here was in a good mood. After the battles, some wouldn't be in such good moods, but right now, all were happy and filled with anticipation.

Lying on a chaise beside him was his young protégé, Lord Karramyn Langston. Langston had rich brown hair that matched his dark eyes, a strong, fit body, and a lazy smile. He was also completely devoted to Blackmoore, and was the one human being Blackmoore had told of his ultimate plans. Though many years his junior, Langston shared many of Blackmoore's ideals and lack of scruples. They were a good pair. Langston had fallen asleep in the warm sunshine, and snored softly.

Blackmoore reached over and snagged another bite of roasted fowl and a goblet of red wine, red as the blood that would soon be spilled in the arena, to wash it down with. Life was good, and with every challenge Thrall met and passed, life got even better. After each match, Blackmoore left with a heavy purse. His "pet orc," once the joke of the fortress, was now his pride.

Of course, most of the others that Thrall went up against were nothing more than humans. Some of the meanest, strongest, most cunning humans to be sure, but human nonetheless. The other gladiators were all brutal, hardened convicts hoping to earn their way out of prison by winning money and fame for their patrons. Some did, and earned their freedom. Most found themselves in just another jail, one with tapestries on the wall and women in their beds, but it was a prison nonetheless. Few patrons wanted to see their money-winners walk as free men.

But some of Thrall's adversaries weren't human, and that was when things got exciting.

It didn't hurt Blackmoore's ambitions at all that the orcs were now a defeated, downtrodden rabble rather than the awesome and fear-inspiring fighting force they had once been. The war was long over, and humans had won the decisive victory. Now the enemy was led into special internment camps almost as easily as cattle into stalls at the end of a day spent grazing. Camps, Blackmoore mused pleasantly, that he was completely in charge of.

At first, his plan was to raise the orc to be a well-educated, loyal slave and a peerless warrior. He would send Thrall to defeat his own people, if "people" was even the proper term for such mindless green thugs, and once they had been defeated, use the broken clans to his, Blackmoore's, own purpose.

But the Horde had been defeated by the Alliance without Thrall having even tasted battle. At first, Blackmoore had been sour about this. But then another thought came to him on how he could use his pet orc. It required patience, something Blackmoore had only in short supply, but the rewards would be far greater than he could have imagined. Infighting was already rampant among the Alliance. Elf sneered at human, human mocked dwarf, and dwarf mistrusted elf. A nice little triangle of bigotry and suspicion.

He raised himself from his chair long enough to observe Thrall defeat one of the biggest, nastiest-looking men Blackmoore had ever seen. But the human warrior was no match for the unstoppable green beast. The cheers went up, and Blackmoore smiled. He waved Tammis Foxton over, and the servant hastened to obey.

"My lord?"

"How many is that today?" Blackmoore knew his voice was slurred but he didn't care. Tammis had seen him drunker than this. Tammis had put him to *bed* drunker than this.

Tammis's prim, anxious face looked even more concerned than usual. "How many what, my lord?" His gaze flickered to the bottle, then back to Blackmoore.

Sudden rage welled up in Blackmoore. He grabbed Tammis by the shirtfront and yanked him down to within an inch of his face.

"Counting the bottles, you pathetic excuse for a man?" he hissed, keeping his voice low. One of the many threats he held over Tammis was public disgrace; even drunk as Blackmoore was, he didn't want to play that particular card quite yet. But he threatened it often, as now. Before his slightly swimmy vision he saw Tammis pale. "You farm out your own wife to suckle monsters, and you dare imply that I have weaknesses?"

Sickened by the man's pasty face, he shoved him away. "I wanned to know how many rounds Thrall has won."

"Oh, yes, sir, of course. Half dozen, all in a row." Tammis paused, looking utterly miserable. "With all due respect, sir, this last one taxed him. Are you sure you want to put him through three more matches?"

Idiots. Blackmoore was surrounded by idiots. When Sergeant had read the order of battles this morning, he, too, had confronted Blackmoore, saying the orc needed at least a few moments of rest, and couldn't they switch the combatant list so that the poor coddled creature could relax.

"Oh, no. The odds against Thrall go higher with ever' battle. He's never lost, not once. Of course I want to stop and give all those nice people their money back." Disgusted, he waved Tammis away. Thrall was incapable of being defeated. Why not make hay while the sun shone?

Thrall won the next battle, but even Blackmoore could see the creature struggling. He adjusted his chair for a better view. Langston imitated him. The battle after that, the eighth of the nine for which the orc was scheduled, saw something that Blackmoore and the crowds had never witnessed.

The mighty orc was tiring. The combatants this time were a pair of mountain cats, caught two weeks ago, penned, tormented, and barely fed until this moment. Once the door to the arena slid open they exploded at the orc as if they had been fired from a cannon. Their creamy brown pelts were a blur as, moving as one, they leaped on him, and Thrall went down beneath their claws and teeth.

A horrified cry arose among the onlookers. Blackmoore sprang to his feet, and immediately had to seize his chair in order to keep from falling down. All that money. . . .

And then Thrall was up! Screaming in rage, shaking the big animals off him as if they were but tree squirrels, he used the two swords that were his assigned weapon in this fight with speed and skill. Thrall was completely ambidextrous, and the blades sparkled in the bright sunlight as they whirled and slashed. One cat was already dead, its long, lithe body sliced nearly in two by a single powerful stroke. The remaining animal, goaded to further rage by the death of its mate, attacked with renewed fury. This time Thrall did not give it an opening. When the cat sprang, all yowls and claws and teeth, Thrall was ready for it. His sword sliced left, right, and left again. The cat fell in four bloody chunks.

"Will you look at that?" said Langston happily.

The crowd roared its approval. Thrall, who normally welcomed the cries with raised fists and stamped his feet almost until the earth itself shook, merely stood there with stooped shoulders. He was breathing raggedly, and Blackmoore saw that the cats had left their mark with several deep, bleeding scratches and bites. As he stared at his prized slave, Thrall slowly turned his ugly head and looked straight up at Blackmoore. Their eyes met, and in their depths Blackmoore saw agony and exhaustion . . . and an unspoken plea.

Then Thrall, the mighty warrior, fell to his knees. Again the crowd reacted vocally. Blackmoore fancied he even heard sympathy in the sound. Langston said nothing, but his brown eyes were watching Blackmoore intently.

Damn Thrall! He was an orc, had been fighting since he was six years old. Most of his matches today had been with humans, mighty warriors to be sure, but nothing to compare with Thrall's brute strength. This was a ploy to get out of the final round, which Thrall knew would be the toughest of all. Selfish, stupid slave. Wanted to go back to his cozy cell, read his books, and eat his food, did he? Well, Blackmoore would teach *him* a thing or two.

At that moment, Sergeant trotted onto the field. "Lord Blackmoore!" he cried, cupping his hands around his bearded mouth. "Will you cede this last challenge?"

Heat flared on Blackmoore's cheeks. How dare Sergeant do this, in front of everyone! Blackmoore, who was still standing unsteadily, gripped the back of the chair harder with his left hand. Langston moved unobtrusively to offer aid if he needed it. Blackmoore extended his right hand straight out in front of him, then brought the hand over to his left shoulder.

No.

Sergeant stared at him for a moment, as if he couldn't believe what he was seeing. Then, he nodded, and signaled that this final bout would begin.

Thrall climbed to his feet, looking as if he had a ton of stones on his back. Several men scurried onto the field, to remove the dead mountain cats and dropped weapons. They handed Thrall the weapon that he was to use for this battle: the morningstar, a studded, metal ball attached by a chain to a thick stick. Thrall took the weapon, and tried to draw himself up into a threatening posture. Even at this distance Blackmoore could see that he trembled. Usually, before each battle, Thrall stamped on the earth. The steady rhythm both excited the crowd and seemed to help Thrall feel more ready for combat. Today, though, he simply seemed struggling to stay on his feet.

One more bout. The creature could handle that.

The doors opened, but for a moment, nothing emerged from the inner gloom.

Then it came, its two heads crying incoherent challenges, its pale body towering over Thrall as Thrall towered over humans. It had only one weapon, as Thrall did, but it was a superior one for this battle—a long, deadly-looking spear. Between the length of its arms and the shaft of the spear, the ogre would be able to reach Thrall from much farther away. Thrall would need to get in close in order to strike any kind of a blow, let alone a winning one.

This was so unfair! "Who gave the ogre that spear?" Blackmoore bellowed to Langston. "It ought to have something at least similar to what Thrall has been given!" Blackmoore conveniently chose not to remember all the times that Thrall had been equipped with a broadsword or spear himself and his human opponents had had to make do with a short sword or ax.

The ogre marched into the circular arena like a machine of war rather than a living, breathing being. He stabbed forward with his spear, one head turned toward the crowd, one head facing Thrall.

Thrall had never seen one of these creatures before, and for a moment simply stood, staring at it. Then he rallied, drew himself up to his full height, and began to swing the morningstar. He threw back his head, tangled long black hair brushing his back, and let loose with a howl to match the ogre's bellowing.

The ogre charged, stabbing forward with the spear. There was no finesse in his movements, only brute strength. Thrall easily ducked the clumsy charge, slipped underneath the ogre's defenses, and swung hard with the morningstar. The ogre cried out and slowed as the spiked ball struck him heavily in the midsection. Thrall had dashed past and now whirled to attack again.

Before the ogre could even turn around, Thrall had struck him in the back. The ogre fell to his knees, dropping the spear and reaching to clutch his back.

Blackmoore smiled. Surely that had broken the miserable creature's spine. These fights weren't necessarily to the death—in fact, killing one's opponent was frowned on as it reduced the pool of good fighters—but everyone knew that dying was a very real possibility in this ring. Healers and their salves couldn't fix everything. And Blackmoore couldn't manage to find any sympathy at all for an ogre.

But his pleasure was short-lived. Even as Thrall began to swing the morningstar again, gathering momentum, the ogre lurched to his feet and seized the dropped spear. Thrall swung the morningstar at the creature's head. To the crowd's amazement, and obviously to Thrall's as well, the ogre simply extended a big hand and batted the spike out of the way while shoving forward with the spear.

The morningstar flew from Thrall's hand. He was knocked off balance and could not recover in time. Even as he desperately tried to twist out of the way the spear impaled him high in the chest, a few inches from his left shoulder. He screamed in agony. The ogre continued to shove as he approached, and the spear went completely through Thrall's body. He fell backward, and was pinned to the earth. Now the ogre fell atop him, pummeling the hapless orc madly and uttering horrible grunts and squeals.

Blackmoore stared in horror. The orc was being beaten, as helpless as a child beneath the onslaught of a bully. The gladiator ring, a showcase for the finest warriors in the kingdom to compete against one another using strength, skill, and cunning, had been reduced to nothing more than one weak monster being beaten to a pulp by another, bigger one.

How could Thrall have let this happen?

Men now hastened onto the field. With sharpened sticks, they prodded the ogre, trying to goad him into leaving off his prey. The brute responded to the taunts, abandoning a bloody Thrall and chasing after the men. Three others tossed a magical net, which immediately shrank to engulf the raging ogre and compress his flailing limbs close to his body. He thrashed now like a fish out of water, and the men, not at all gently, hauled the creature onto a cart and took him out of the ring.

Thrall, too, was being carried out, though with much more gentleness. Blackmoore's patronage assured that. But Blackmoore realized that he had lost every penny he had bet on Thrall today because of this single fight. Many of his companions had done likewise, and he could feel the heat of their furious glares as they reached for their purses to pay their debts.

Thrall. Thrall. *Thrall.* . . .

Thrall lay gasping on the straw that served him as a bed. He had never known such pain existed. Nor such exhaustion. He wished he would fall unconscious; it would be so much easier.

Nonetheless, he would not let the welcoming blackness overtake him. The healers would be here soon; Blackmoore always sent them after Thrall had been injured in a bout. Blackmoore also always came to visit him, and Thrall eagerly awaited the comforting words of his master. He had lost the battle, true, and that was a first, but surely Blackmoore would have nothing but praise for how well he had fought nine bouts in a row. That was unheard of, Thrall knew. Thrall also knew he could have beaten the ogre if he had been matched against him in the first bout, or the third, or even the sixth. But no one could expect him to win after a record-breaking eight bouts.

He closed his eyes as pain seared him. The hot burning in his chest was nigh unbearable. Where were the healers? They should have been here by now. He knew his injuries were bad this time. He estimated he had several broken ribs, a broken leg, several sword slashes, and of course the dreadful hole in his shoulder where the spear had impaled him. They would have to come soon if Thrall were to be able to fight again tomorrow.

Thrall heard the lock open, but could not lift his head to see who entered his cell.

"The healers will be here," came Blackmoore's voice. Thrall tensed. The voice was slurred and dripped with contempt. His heart began to speed up. Please, not this time . . . not now. . . .

"But they won't be here anytime soon. I wan' see you suffer, you poxy son of a whore."

And then Thrall gasped in torment as Blackmoore's boot kicked him in the stomach. The pain was incredible, but not nearly as searing as the shock of betrayal that shuddered through him. Why would Blackmoore strike him when he was so badly injured? Did he not see how well Thrall had fought?

Though the pain threatened to cause him to lose consciousness, Thrall raised his head and stared at Blackmoore with blurred vision. The man's face was contorted in anger, and even as Thrall met his eyes Blackmoore struck him soundly across the face with a mailed fist. Everything went black for an instant and when Thrall could next hear, Blackmoore was still railing.

". . . lost thousands, do you hear me, *thousands!* What is the matter with you? It was one pathetic little fight!"

He was still raining blows on Thrall, but Thrall was starting to drift away. He felt as if his body only vaguely belonged to him, and the kicks Blackmoore delivered felt more and more like taps. He felt blood sticky on his face.

Blackmoore had seen him. He knew how exhausted Thrall had been, had watched him rally again and again and again to hold his own eight out of nine times. There was no way anyone could have expected Thrall to win that fight. Thrall had fought with everything he had, and he had lost fairly and honorably. And yet that was not good enough for Blackmoore.

Finally, the blows stopped. He heard the steps as Blackmoore left, and a single phrase: "Let the others have their turn."

The door did not close. Thrall heard more footsteps. He could not raise his head again, though he tried. Several pairs of black military boots appeared in front of him. Thrall now realized what Blackmoore had ordered. One boot drew back slightly, then swung forward, kicking Thrall in the face.

His world went white, then black; then he knew no more.

Thrall awoke to warmth and a cessation of the agony that had been his companion for what seemed like an eternity. Three healers were working on him, using their salve to heal his wounds. Breathing was much easier and he guessed his ribs had been healed. They were administering the sweet-smelling, gooey stuff to his shoulder now; clearly that was the most difficult wound.

Although their touches were gentle, and their salve brought healing, there was no real compassion in these men. They healed him because Blackmoore paid them to do so, not out of any real desire to ease suffering. Once, he had been more naive and had thanked them sincerely for their efforts. One of them looked up, startled at the words.

A sneer had curled his lip. "Don't flatter yourself, monster. Once the coins stop flowing, so does the salve. Better not lose."

He had winced from the unkind words then, but they did not bother him now. Thrall understood. He understood many things. It was as if his vision had been cloudy, and a thick fog had suddenly lifted. He lay quietly until they had finished; then they rose and left.

Thrall sat upright and was surprised to see Sergeant

standing there, his hairy arms folded across his broad chest. Thrall did not speak, wondering what new torment was coming.

"I pulled 'em off you," said Sergeant quietly. "But not before they'd had their sport. Blackmoore had some . . . business . . . he needed to talk w' me about. I'm sorry for that, lad. I'm right sorry. You amazed me in the ring today. Blackmoore ought to be prouder'n hell 'o you. Instead. . . ." His gruff voice trailed off. "Well, I wanted to make sure you knew that you didn't deserve what he did. What they did. You did fine, lad. Just fine. Better get some sleep."

He seemed about to say something more, then nodded and left. Thrall lay back down, absently noting that they had changed the straw. It was fresh and clean, no longer clotted with his blood.

He appreciated what Sergeant had done, and believed the man. But it was too little, too late.

He would not let himself be used like this any longer. Once, he would have cringed and vowed to be better, to do something to earn the love and respect he so desperately craved. Now, he knew he would never find it here, not as long as Blackmoore owned him.

He would not sleep. He would use this time to plan. He reached for the tablet and stylus he kept in the sack, and wrote a note to the only person he could trust: Tari.

On the next dark moons, I plan to escape.

SIX

The grate above his head allowed Thrall to observe the moonslight. He was careful to give no hint, not to the trainees who had beaten him, not to Sergeant, and certainly not to Blackmoore (who treated Thrall as if nothing had happened) about his profound revelation. He was as obsequious as ever, for the first time noticing how he hated himself for that behavior. He kept his eyes lowered, although he knew himself to be the equal of any human. He went docilely into the irons, though he could have torn any four guards to bloody bits before they could have restrained him without his cooperation. In no way did he change his behavior, not in the cell nor out of it, not in the ring nor on the training field.

For the first day or two, Thrall noticed Sergeant watching him sharply, as if expecting to see the changes Thrall was determined not to show. But he did not speak to Thrall, and Thrall was careful not to arouse suspicion. Let them think they had broken him. His only regret was that he would not be present to see the look on Blackmoore's face when he discovered his "pet orc" had flown.

For the first time in his life, Thrall had something to look forward to with anticipation. It roused a hunger in him he had never known before. He had always concentrated so intensely on avoiding beatings and earning praise that he had never permitted himself to really think long and hard about what it meant to be free. To walk in the sunlight without chains, to sleep under the stars. He had never been outside at night in his life. What would that be like?

His imagination, fueled by books and by letters from Tari, was finally allowed to fly. He lay awake in his straw bed wondering what it would be like to finally meet one of his people. He had read, of course, all the information the humans had on "the vile green monsters from the blackest demon pits." And there was that disturbing incident when the orc had wrenched himself free to charge Thrall. If only he could have found out what the orc was saying! But his rudimentary orcish did not extend that far.

He would learn, one day, what that orc had said. He would find his people. Thrall might have been raised by humans, but little enough had been done to win his love and loyalty. He was grateful to Sergeant and Tari, for they had taught him concepts of honor and kindness. But because of their teachings, Thrall better understood Blackmoore, and realized that the Lieutenant General had none of those qualities. And as long as Thrall was owned by him, the orc would never receive them in his own life.

The moons, one large and silver and one smaller and a shade of blue-green, were new tonight. Tari had responded to his declaration with an offer to assist him, as he had known in his heart she would. Between the two of them, they had been able to come up with a plan that had a strong likelihood of working. But he did not know when that plan would go into effect, and so he waited for the signal. And waited.

He had fallen into a fitful slumber when the clanging of a bell startled him awake. Instantly alert, he went to the farthest wall of his cell. Over the years, Thrall had painstakingly worked a single stone loose and had hollowed out the space behind it. It was here that he stored his most precious things: his letters from Tari. Now he moved the stone, found the letters, and wrapped them up in the only other thing that meant anything to him, his swaddling cloth with the white wolf against the blue field. For a brief moment, he held them to his chest. Then he turned, and awaited his chance.

The bell continued to ring, and now shouts and screams joined it. Thrall's sensitive nose, much more keen than a human's, could smell smoke. The smell grew stronger with each heartbeat, and now he could see a faint orange and yellow lightening of the darkness of his cell.

"Fire!" came the cries. "Fire!"

Not knowing why, Thrall leaped for his makeshift bed. He closed his eyes and feigned sleep, forcing his rapid breathing to become deep and slow.

"He's not going anywhere," said one of the guards. Thrall knew he was being watched. He kept up the illusion of deep sleep. "Heh. Damned monster could sleep through anything. Come on, let's give them a hand."

"I don't know. . . ." said the other one.

More cries of alarm, mixed now with the treble shrieks of children and the high voices of women.

"It's spreading," said the first one. "Come *on!*"

Thrall heard the sounds of boots striking hard stone. The sounds receded. He was alone.

He rose, and stood in front of the huge wooden door. Of course it was still locked, but there was no one to see what he was about to do.

Thrall took a deep breath, then with a rush of speed charged the door, striking it with his left shoulder. It gave, but not entirely. Again he struck, and again. Five times he had to slam his enormous body against it before the old timbers surrendered with a crash. The momentum carried him forward and he landed heavily on the floor, but the brief pain was as nothing compared to the surge of excitement he experienced.

He knew these hallways. He had no problem seeing in the dim light provided by the few torches positioned in sconces that were fastened here and there to the stone walls. Down this one, up this stairwell, and then. . . .

As it had earlier in his cell, a deep instinct kicked in. He flattened himself against the wall, hiding his huge form in the shadows as best he could. From across the entryway, several more guards charged. They did not see him, and Thrall let his held breath out in a sigh of relief.

The guards left the door to the courtyard wide open. Cautiously Thrall approached, and peered out.

All was chaos. The barns were almost completely engulfed by flames, though the horses, goats, and donkeys ran panic-stricken in the courtyard. This was even better, for there was less chance of him being spotted in the milling madness. A bucket chain had been formed, and even as Thrall watched, several more men hastened up, spilling the precious water in their heedless rush.

Thrall looked to the right of the courtyard gate entrance. Lying in a crumpled pool of black was the object he was seeking: a huge black cloak. Even as large as it was, it could not possibly cover him, but it would serve. He covered his head and broad chest, crouched so that the short hem would fall lower on his legs, and scurried forward.

The trip across the courtyard to the main gates could not have lasted more than a few moments, but to Thrall it seemed an eternity. He tried to keep his head low, but he had to look up frequently in order to avoid being run down by a cart carrying barrels of rainwater, or a maddened horse, or a screaming child. His heart pounding, he threaded his way amid the chaos. He could feel the heat, and the bright light of the fire lit up the entire scene almost as brightly as the sun did. Thrall concentrated on putting one foot in front of the other, keeping as low as possible, and heading for the gates.

Finally, he made it. These, too, had been thrown open. More carts carrying rain barrels clattered through, the drivers having a hard time controlling their frightened mounts. No one noticed one lone figure slipping out into the darkness.

Once clear of the fortress, Thrall ran. He headed straight for the surrounding forested hills, leaving the road as soon as possible. His senses seemed sharper than they had ever been. Unfamiliar scents filled his flaring nostrils, and it felt as if he could sense every rock, every blade of grass beneath his running feet.

There was a rock formation that Taretha had told him about. She said it looked a bit like a dragon standing guard over the forest. It was very dark, but Thrall's excellent night vision could make out a jut that, if one used one's imagination, could indeed appear to be the long neck of a reptilian creature. There was a cave here, Taretha said. He would be safe.

For the briefest moment, he wondered if Taretha might not be setting a trap for him. At once he dismissed the idea, both angry and ashamed that it had even occurred to him. Taretha had been nothing but kind to him via her supportive letters. Why would she betray him? And more to the point, why go to such great lengths when simply showing his letters to Blackmoore would accomplish the same thing?

There it was, a dark oval against the gray face of the stone. Thrall was not even breathing heavily as he altered his course and trotted for the refuge.

He could see her inside, leaning against the cave wall, waiting for him. For a moment he paused, knowing that his vision was superior to hers. Even though she was within and he without, she could not see him.

Thrall had only human values by which to measure beauty, and he could tell that, by those standards, Taretha Foxton was lovely. Long pale hair—it was too dark for him to see the exact color, but he had glimpsed her momentarily in the stands at the matches from time to time—fell in a long braid down her back. She was clad only in nightclothes, a cloak wrapped close about her slender frame, and beside her was a large sack.

He paused for a moment, and then strode boldly up to her. "Taretha," he said, his voice deep and gruff.

She gasped and looked up at him. He thought her afraid, but then she laughed. "You startled me! I did not know you moved so quietly!" The laughter faded, settled into a smile. She strode forward and reached out both hands to him.

Slowly, Thrall folded them in his own. The small white hands disappeared in his green ones, nearly three times as large. Taretha barely reached his elbow, yet there was no fear on her face, only pleasure.

"I could kill you where you stand," he said, wondering what perverse emotion was making him say those words. "No witnesses that way."

Her smile only grew. "Of course you could," she acknowledged, her voice warm and melodious. "But you won't."

"How do you know?"

"Because I know *you.*" He opened his hands and released her. "Did you have any trouble?"

"None," he said. "The plan worked well. There was so much chaos that I think an entire village of orcs could have escaped. I noticed that you released the animals before setting fire to the barn."

She grinned again. Her nose turned up slightly, making her look younger than her—what, twenty? Twenty-five?—years.

"Of course. They're just innocent creatures. I'd never want to see them harmed. Now, we had best hurry." She looked down at Durnholde, at the smoke and flames still billowing up into the starry sky. "They seem to be getting control of it. You'll be missed soon." An emotion Thrall didn't understand shadowed her face for a moment. "As will I." She took the sack and brought it out into the open. "Sit, sit. I want to show you something."

Obediently, he sat down. Tari rummaged through the sack and withdrew a scroll. Unrolling it, she held it down on one side and gestured that he do the same.

"It's a map," said Thrall.

"Yes, the most accurate one I could find. Here's Durnholde," said Taretha, pointing at a drawing of a small castlelike building. "We're slightly to the southwest, right here. The internment camps are all within a twenty-mile radius of Durnholde, here, here, here, here, and here." She pointed to drawings so small even Thrall couldn't quite make them out in the poor light. "Your best chance for safety is to go here, into the wilderness area. I've heard that there are still some of your people hiding out there, but Blackmoore's men are never able to find them, just traces." She looked up at him. "You'll somehow need to find them, Thrall. Get them to help you."

Your people, Taretha had said. Not *the orcs,* or *those things,* or *those monsters.* Gratitude suddenly welled up inside him so powerfully that for a moment he couldn't speak. Finally, he managed, "Why are you doing this? Why do you want to help me?"

She looked at him steadily, not flinching from what she saw. "Because I remember you when you were a baby. You were like a little brother to me. When . . . when Faralyn died soon afterward, you were the only little brother I had anymore. I saw what they did to you, and I hated it. I wanted to help you, be your friend." Now she looked away. "And I have no more fondness for our master than you do."

"Has he hurt you?" The outrage that Thrall felt surprised him.

"No. Not really." One hand went to the other wrist, massaged it gently. Beneath the sleeve Thrall could see the fading shadow of a bruise. "Not physically. It's more complicated than that."

"Tell me."

"Thrall, time is—"

"Tell me!" he boomed. "You have been my friend, Taretha. For over ten years you have written me, made me smile. I knew someone knew who I really was, not just some . . . some monster in the gladiator ring. You were a light in the darkness." With all the gentleness he could muster, he reached out and placed his hand oh so lightly on her shoulder. "Tell me," he urged again, his voice soft.

Her eyes grew shiny. As he watched, liquid spilled from them and poured down her cheeks. "I'm so ashamed," she whispered.

"What is happening to your eyes?" asked Thrall. "What is 'ashamed'?"

"Oh, Thrall," she said, her voice thick. She wiped at her eyes. "These are called tears. They come when we are so sad, so soul sick, it's as if our hearts are so full of pain there's no place else for it to go." Taretha took a shuddering breath. "And shame . . . it's when you've done something that's so contrary to who you believe yourself to be you wish that no one ever knew about it. But everyone knows, so you might as well, too. I am Blackmoore's mistress."

"What does that mean?"

She regarded him sadly. "You are so innocent, Thrall. So pure. But someday you will understand."

Suddenly Thrall recalled snippets of bragging conversations he had overheard on the training field, and understood what Taretha meant. But he did not feel shame for her, only outrage that Blackmoore had stooped even lower than Thrall had guessed he could. He understood what it was to be helpless before Blackmoore, and Taretha was so small and fragile she couldn't even fight.

"Come with me," he urged.

"I cannot. What he would do to my family if I fled . . . no." She reached out impulsively and gripped his hands. "But you can. Please, go now. I will rest the easier knowing that you, at least, have escaped him. Be free, for the both of us."

He nodded, unable to speak. He had known he would miss her, but now, having actually conversed with Tari, the pain of their parting cut even more deeply.

She wiped her face again and spoke in a steadier voice. "I've packed this full of food and put in several full water skins as well. I was able to steal a knife for you. I didn't dare take anything else that might be missed. Finally, I want you to have this." She bowed her head and removed a silver chain from her long neck. Dangling from the delicate chain was a crescent moon. "Not far from here, there is an old tree that was split by lightning. Blackmoore gives me leave to wander here when I wish. For that, at least, I'm grateful. If you are ever here and in need, place this necklace in the trunk of the old tree, and I will again meet you in this cave and do what I can to help you."

"Tari. . . ." Thrall looked at her miserably.

"Hurry." She cast an anxious glance back at Durnholde. "I have made up a story to excuse my absence, but it will go easier for me the sooner I return." They rose, and looked at one another awkwardly. Before Thrall realized what had happened, Tari had stepped forward and stretched her arms about his massive torso as far as they would reach. Her face pressed against his stomach. Thrall tensed; all such contact hitherto had been as an attack. But although he had never been touched in this way before, he knew it was a sign of affection. Following his instincts, he tentatively patted her head and stroked her hair.

"They call you a monster," she said, her voice thick again as she stepped away from him. "But they're the monsters, not you. Farewell, Thrall."

Taretha turned away, lifted her skirts, and began to run back toward Durnholde. Thrall stood and watched her until she had disappeared from view. Then, with the utmost care, he placed the precious silver necklace in his bundle, then stashed it in the sack.

He lifted the heavy sack—it must have been very difficult for Taretha to carry it so far—and slung it over his back. Then, Thrall, the former slave, began to stride to his destiny.

SEVEN

Thrall knew that Taretha had pointed out where the internment camps were located specifically so that he could avoid them. She wanted him to try to find free orcs. But he was uncertain as to whether these "free orcs" were even still alive or merely figments of some wistful warrior's imagination. He had studied maps while under Jaramin's tutelage, so he knew how to read the one Tari had given him.

And he set a course straight for one of the camps.

He did not choose the one nearest Durnholde; there was a good chance that, once he was missed, Blackmoore would have issued an alert. There was one that, according to the map, was located several leagues away from the fortress where Thrall had reached maturity. This was the one he would visit.

He knew only a little about the camps, and that little

was filtered through the minds of men who hated his people. As he jogged easily and tirelessly toward his destination, his mind raced. What would it be like, to see so many orcs all in one place? Would they be able to understand his speech? Or would it be so tainted with a human accent he would be unable to converse at even the most basic level? Would they challenge him? He did not wish to fight them, but everything he knew told him that orcs were fierce, proud, unstoppable warriors. He was a trained fighter, but would that be enough against one of these legendary beings? Would he be able to hold his own long enough to persuade them that he was not their enemy?

Miles fell beneath his feet. From time to time he looked at the stars to judge his position. He had never been taught how to navigate, but one of the secret books Tari had sent him had dealt with the stars and their positions. Thrall had studied it eagerly, absorbing every scrap of information that had come his way.

Maybe he would meet the clan who bore the emblem of the white wolf head against the blue background. Maybe he would find his family. Blackmoore had told him he had been found not terribly far from Durnholde, so Thrall thought it quite possible that he would encounter members of his clan.

Excitement flooded him. It was good.

He traveled all that night and halted to rest once the sun began to rise. If he knew Blackmoore, and he did, the Lieutenant General would have men out looking for him. Perhaps they would even press into use one of their famed flying machines. Thrall had never seen one, and had privately doubted their existence. But if they did indeed exist, then Blackmoore would commandeer the use of one to find his wandering champion.

He thought of Tari, and desperately hoped that her part in his escape had not been discovered.

Blackmoore did not think he had ever been angrier in his entire life, and that was saying a great deal.

He had been roused from his slumber—alone tonight, Taretha had pleaded illness—by the clamor of the bells and stared in horror out his window at the billowing orange flames across the courtyard. Throwing on clothing, he had raced to join the rest of Durnholde's populace as they frantically tried to contain the blaze. It had taken several hours, but by the time dawn's pink hue had begun to taint the night sky the inferno had been tamed to a pile of sullen embers.

"It's a miracle no one was hurt," said Langston, wiping his forehead. His pale face was tinted black by the soot. Blackmoore fancied he looked no better. Everyone present was soiled and sweaty. The servants would have quite a bit of washing to do tomorrow.

"Not even the animals," said Tammis, coming up to them. "There was no way the animals could have escaped on their own. We can't be certain, my lord, but it's beginning to look as though this fire was deliberately set."

"By the Light!" gasped Langston. "Do you really think so? Who would want to do such a thing?"

"I'd count all my enemies on my hands, except I'd run out of fingers," growled Blackmoore. "And toes. Plenty of bastards out there jealous of my rank and my . . . Lothar's ghost." He suddenly felt cold and imagined that his face was white beneath the soot. Langston and Tammis both stared at him.

He couldn't spare the time to voice his concern. He leaped up from the stone steps upon which he'd been sitting and sped back toward the fortress. Both friend and servant followed him, crying out, "Blackmoore, wait!" and "My lord, what is it?"

Blackmoore ignored them. He hastened down the corridors, up the stairs, and skidded to a halt in front of the broken wooden shards that had once been the door to Thrall's cell. His worst fear had been proven right.

"Damn them all to hell!" he cried. "Someone stole my orc! Tammis! I want men, I want horses, I want flying machines—I want Thrall back immediately!"

Thrall was surprised at how deeply he slept, and how lively his dreams were. He woke as night was falling, and for a moment simply lay where he was. He felt the soft grass beneath his body, enjoyed the breeze that caressed his face. This was freedom, and it was sweet indeed. Precious. He now understood why some would rather die than live imprisoned.

A spear prodded his neck, and the faces of six human males peered down on him.

"You," one of them said, "Get up."

Thrall cursed himself as he was dragged behind a horse, with two men walking guard on either side. How could he have been so foolish! He had wanted to see the encampments, yes, but from the safety of hiding. He wanted to be an observer, not a participant in this system about which he had heard nothing good.

He'd tried to run, but four of them had horses and had run him down almost immediately. They had nets, spears, and swords, and Thrall was ashamed at how quickly and efficiently they managed to render him harmless. He thought about struggling, but decided not to. He was under no illusions that these men would pay for a healing if he were injured, and he wanted to keep his strength up. Also, would there be a better way to meet orcs than to be at the camp with them? Certainly, given their fierce warriors' nature, they would be eager to escape. He had knowledge that could help them.

So he pretended to be overcome, although he could have taken on all of them at once. He regretted his decision almost immediately when the men began to rummage through his sack.

"Plenty of food here," said one. "Good stuff, too. We'll eat well tonight, lads!"

"It's Major Remka who'll be eating well," said another.

"Not if she don't know about it, and we aren't going to tell her," said a third. As Thrall watched, the one who had spoken first bit eagerly into one of the small meat pies Taretha had packed.

"Well, look here," said the second one. "A knife." He rose and went to Thrall, who was helplessly bound in a trap-net. "Stole all this, didn't you?" He thrust the knife at Thrall's face. Thrall didn't even blink.

"Come off it, Hult," said the second man, who was the smallest and most anxious of the six. The others had tied their horses to nearby branches and were busily divvying up the spoils, putting them in their saddlebags and not choosing to report it to the mysterious Major Remka, whoever he was.

"I'm keeping this one," said Hult.

"You can have the food, but you know that everything else we find we really have to report," said the second man, looking nervous about standing up to Hult but doggedly determined to follow orders.

"And what if I don't?" said Hult. Thrall did not like him; he looked mean and angry, like Blackmoore. "What are you going to do about it?"

"It's what I'm going to do about it that ought to concern you, Hult," said a new voice. This man was tall and slender. He did not look physically imposing, but Thrall had fought enough fine warriors to know that often technique was as good as, and sometimes better than, size.

Judging by Hult's reactions, this man was respected. "The rules exist so that we can keep an eye on the orcs. This is the first one we've seen in years that's carried a human weapon. It's worth reporting. As for these. . . ."

Thrall watched in horror as the man began to leaf through Taretha's letters. Blue eyes narrowing, the tall man turned to look at Thrall. "Don't suppose you can read, can you?"

The other men erupted with laughter, crumbs spraying from their mouths, but the man asking the question appeared to be serious. Thrall started to answer, then thought better of it. Better to pretend not to even know the human language, he thought.

The tall man strode up to him. Thrall tensed, anticipating a blow, but instead the man squatted down beside him and stared directly into Thrall's eyes. Thrall looked away.

"You. Read?" The man pointed with a gloved finger to the letters. Thrall stared at them, and, figuring even an orc who didn't speak the human tongue would have made the connection, shook his head violently. The man gazed at him a moment more, then rose. Thrall wasn't sure he'd convinced him.

"He looks familiar, somehow," said the man. Thrall went cold inside.

"They all look the same to me," said Hult. "Big, green, and ugly."

"Too bad none of us can read," said the man. "I bet these papers would tell us a lot."

"You're always dreaming above your station, Waryk," said Hult, a hint of contempt in his voice.

Waryk shoved the letters back into the sack, plucked the knife from Hult's grasp over the man's halfhearted protest, and slung the now mostly-empty sack over his horse's withers. "Put the food away, before I change my mind. Let's take him to the camp."

Thrall had assumed they would put him on a cart, or perhaps in one of the wagons he remembered from so long ago. He was not granted even that basest of courtesies. They simply attached a rope to the trap-net that bound his limbs so tightly and dragged him behind one of their horses. Thrall, however, had an extremely high pain threshold after so many years in the gladiator ring. What hurt him more deeply was the loss of Taretha's letters. It was fortunate that none of these men could read. He was grateful they had not found the necklace. He had been holding the necklace she'd given him last night and had managed to slip it inside his black trousers before it was noticed. That part of her, at least, he could still hold on to.

The journey seemed to take forever, but the sun crawled across the sky only slowly. Finally, they reached a large stone wall. Waryk called for admittance, and Thrall heard what sounded like heavy gates opening. He was being dragged on his back, so he had an excellent view of the thickness of the wall as they entered. Disinterested guards threw the newcomer a brief glance, then went about their business.

The first thing that struck Thrall was the stench. It reminded him of the stables at Durnholde, but was much stronger. He wrinkled his nose. Hult was watching it and he laughed.

"Been away from your own kind too long, eh, greenie?" he sneered. "Forgotten how bad you smell?" He pinched his nose shut and rolled his eyes.

"Hult," said Waryk, a warning in his voice. He grasped the net's webbing and spoke a word of command. At once Thrall felt his bonds loosen and he got to his feet.

He stared about in horror. Huddled everywhere were dozens—perhaps hundreds— of orcs. Some sat in puddles of their own filth, their eyes unfocused, their sharp-tusked jaws slack. Others paced back and forth, muttering incoherently. Some slept tightly curled up on the earth, seeming not to care even if they were stepped on. There was an occasional squabble, but even that apparently sapped too much energy, for it died down almost as quickly as it had begun.

What was going on here? Were these men drugging Thrall's people? That had to be the answer. He knew what orcs were, how fierce, how savage. He had expected . . . well, he had not known what to expect, but certainly not this peculiar, unnatural lethargy.

"Go on," said Waryk, shoving Thrall gently toward the nearest cluster of orcs. "Food's put out once a day. There's water in the troughs."

Thrall stood up straight and tried to put a bold face
on it as he strode to a group of five orcs, sitting beside
the aforementioned water troughs. He could feel
Waryk's eyes boring into his scraped and bruised back
and heard the man say, "I could swear I've seen him
somewhere before." Then he heard the men walking
away.

Only one of the orcs looked up as Thrall approached. His heart was racing. He had never been this
close to one of his people before, and now, here were
five of them.

"I greet you," he said in orcish.

They stared at him. One of them looked down and
resumed clawing at a small rock embedded in the dirt.

Thrall tried again. "I greet you," he said, spreading
his arms in the gesture that the books told him indicated one warrior saluting another.

"Where'd they catch you?" one of them finally
asked, speaking the human language. At Thrall's startled look, she said, "You weren't raised to speak orcish.
I can tell."

"You're right. I was raised by humans. They taught
me only a little orcish. I was hoping you could help me
learn more."

The orcs looked at one another, then broke into
laughter. "Raised by humans, eh? Hey, Krakis—come
over here! We got ourselves a good storyteller! All
right, Shaman, tell us another one."

Thrall felt his chance to connect with these people

slipping through his fingers. "Please, I mean no insult. I'm a prisoner like you are now. I've never met any orcs, I just want. . . ."

Now the one who had looked away turned around, and Thrall fell silent. This orc's eyes were bright red and seemed to glow, as if lit from within. "So you want to meet your people? Well, you've met us. Now leave us be." He turned back to picking at the stone.

"Your eyes . . ." Thrall murmured, too stunned by the strange red glow to recognize the insult.

The orc cringed, lifted a hand to shield his face from Thrall's gaze, and hunched away even farther.

Thrall turned to ask a question and found himself standing alone. The other orcs had all shuffled away, casting furtive glances back at him.

The sky had been clouding over all day, and it had steadily been growing colder. Now, as Thrall stood alone in the center of a courtyard surrounded by what remained of his people, the gray skies opened and icy rain mixed with snow began to fall.

Thrall barely noticed the wretched weather, so deep was his personal misery. Was this why he had severed every tie he had ever known? To live out his life as a captive in a group of spiritless, sluggish creatures whom he once dreamed of leading against the tyranny of the humans? Which was worse, he mused, fighting in the ring for the glory of Blackmoore, sleeping safe and dry, reading letters from Tari, or standing here alone, shunned even by those of his own blood, his feet sinking into freezing mud?

The answer came swiftly: Both were intolerable. Without appearing too obvious, Thrall began to look about with an eye toward escape. It should be simple enough. Only a few guards here and there, and at night, they would have more difficulty seeing than Thrall would. They looked bored and disinterested, and judging by the lack of spirit, even energy or interest, displayed by this pathetic collection of orcs, Thrall did not think even one of them would have the courage to try to climb the rather low walls.

He felt the rain now, as it soaked the trousers he wore. A gray, gloomy day, for a gray, gloomy lesson. The orcs were no noble, fierce warriors. He could not imagine how these creatures ever gave the humans the slightest bit of resistance.

"We were not always as you see us here," came a soft, deep voice at his elbow. Surprised, Thrall turned around to see the red-eyed orc staring up at him with those unsettling orbs. "Soulless, afraid, ashamed. This is what *they* did to us," he continued, pointing to his eyes. "And if we could be rid of it, our hearts and spirits might return."

Thrall sank down in the mud beside him. "Go on," he urged. "I'm listening."

EIGHT

It had been almost two days since the fire and Thrall's escape, and Blackmoore had spent the better part of that time angry and brooding. It was at Tammis's urging that he had finally gone out hawking, and he had to admit, his servant had had a good idea.

The day was gloomy, but he and Taretha were well dressed and the vigorous riding kept their blood warm. He had wanted to go hunting, but his softhearted mistress had persuaded him that simply riding would be enough to pleasantly pass the time. He watched her canter past on the pretty dapple gray he had given her two years ago and wished the weather were warmer. He could think of other ways to pleasantly pass the time with Taretha.

What an unexpectedly ripe fruit Foxton's daughter had been. She had been a lovely, obedient child, and had matured into a lovely, obedient woman. Who would have thought those bright blue eyes would snare him so, that he would so love to bury his face in the flowing gold of her long tresses? Not he, not Blackmoore. But since he had taken her for his own several years ago, she had managed to constantly entertain him, a rare feat.

Langston had once inquired when Blackmoore was going to put aside Taretha in favor of a wife. Blackmoore had replied that there would be no putting aside Taretha even when he *did* take a wife, and there was plenty of time for such things when his plan had finally come to fruition. He would be in a much better position to command a politically favorable marriage once he had brought the Alliance to its collective knees.

And truly, there was no rush. There was plenty of time now to enjoy Taretha whenever and wherever he wished. And the more of that time he spent with the girl, the less it was about satisfying his urges and the more it was about simply enjoying her presence. More than once, as he lay awake and watched her sleep, silvered in moonlight streaming through the windows, he wondered if he was falling in love with her.

He had pulled up Nightsong, who was growing older but who still enjoyed a good canter now and then, and was watching her playfully guide Gray Lady in circles around him. At his order, she had not covered nor braided her hair, and it fell loose around her shoulders like a fall of purest gold. Taretha was laughing, and for a moment their eyes met.

To hell with the weather. They would make do.

He was about to order her off her steed and into a nearby copse of trees—their capes would keep them sufficiently warm—when he heard the sound of hoofbeats approaching. He scowled as Langston emerged, panting. His horse was lathered and steaming in the chill afternoon.

"My lord," he gasped, "I believe we have news of Thrall!"

Major Lorin Remka was not a person to be trifled with. Although she stood only a little bit over five feet tall, she was stocky and strong, and could handle herself more than adequately in any fight. She had enlisted disguised as a man many years ago out of a passionate desire to destroy the greenskin beings that had attacked her village. When the subterfuge had been discovered, her commanding officer had put her right back in the front lines. Later, she had learned that the officer had hoped she'd be killed, thus sparing him the embarrassment of reporting her. But Lorin Remka had stubbornly survived, and had acquitted herself as well as, and in some cases better than, any man in her unit.

She had taken a savage pleasure in slaughtering the enemy. In more than one case, after a kill she'd rubbed the reddish-black blood all over her face to mark her victory. The men had always given her a wide berth.

In this time of peace, Major Remka took almost as much pleasure in ordering about the slugs that had once been her direst enemies, although that pleasure had diminished once the bastards ceased to fight back. Why they had become so much more like cattle and less like monsters had often been a subject of discussion between Remka and her men late in the evenings, over a game of cards and an ale or four.

Most satisfying of all had been being able to take these once-terrifying killers and turn them into bowing and scraping servants. She found the ones most malleable who had the odd red eyes. They seemed eager for direction and praise, even from her. Now one of them was drawing a bath for her in her quarters.

"Make sure it's hot, Greekik," she called. "And don't forget the herbs this time!"

"Yes, my lady," called the female orc in a humble voice. Almost immediately, Remka could smell the cleansing scent of the dried herbs and flowers. Ever since she'd been working here, it seemed to her as if she stank all the time. She couldn't get it out of her clothes, but at least she could soak her body in the hot, scented water and wash it from her skin and long black hair.

Remka had adopted the male style of clothing, much more practical than all that feminine frippery. After years spent on the field of battle, she was more than used to dressing herself and actually preferred it. Now she removed her boots with a sigh. Just as she set them aside for Greekik to clean there came an urgent knock on the door.

"This had better be good," she muttered, opening the door. "What is it, Waryk?"

"We captured an orc yesterday," he began.

"Yes, yes, I read your report. My bath is cooling even as we speak and—"

"I thought the orc looked familiar," Waryk pressed.

"By the Light, Waryk, they all look the same!"

"No. This one looked different. And I know why now." He stepped aside, and a tall, imposing figure filled the doorway. Immediately Major Remka snapped to attention, wishing desperately she still had her boots on.

"Lieutenant General Blackmoore," she said. "How may we be of service?"

"Major Remka," said Aedelas Blackmoore, white teeth gleaming through a neatly trimmed black goatee, "I believe you've found my lost pet orc."

Thrall listened, captivated, as the red-eyed orc spoke in a soft voice of tales of valor and strength. He told of charges made against impossible odds, of heroic deeds, and of humans falling beneath a relentless green tide of orcs united in purpose. He spoke wistfully of a spiritual people as well, something Thrall had never heard of.

"Oh, yes," Kelgar said sadly. "Once, before we were the proud, battle-hungry Horde, we were individual clans. And in those clans were those who knew the magic of wind and water, of sky and land, of all the spirits of the wild, and they worked in harmony with those powers. We called them 'shamans,' and until the emergence of the warlocks, their skills were all we knew of power."

The word seemed to make Kelgar angry. He spat and with the first rousing of any kind of passion, snarled, "Power! Does it feed our people, raise our young? Our leaders held it all themselves, and only the barest trickle dripped down to the rest of us. They did . . . something, Thrall. I do not know what. But once we were defeated, all desire to fight bled out of us as if from an open wound." He lowered his head, placing it on arms folded across his knees, and closed his red eyes.

"Did all of you lose the desire to fight?" asked Thrall.

"All of us here. Those who fought weren't captured, or if they were, they were killed as they resisted." Kelgar kept his eyes closed.

Thrall respected the other orc's need for silence. Disappointment filled him. Kelgar's tale had the ring of truth about it, and for verification, all Thrall needed to do was look around him. What was this strange thing that had happened? How could an entire race of people have their natures so distorted as to end up here, defeated before they were even caught and thrown into this wretched hellhole?

"But the desire to fight is still strong in you, Thrall, though your name suggests otherwise." His eyes were open again, and they seemed to burn into Thrall. "Perhaps your being raised by humans spared you this.

There are others like you, still out there. The walls are not so high that you cannot climb them, if that is your wish."

"It is," said Thrall eagerly. "Tell me where I can find others like me."

"The only one I have heard tell of is Grom Hellscream," Kelgar said. "He remains undefeated. His people, the Warsong clan, came from the west of this land. That is all I can tell you. Grom has eyes like me, but his spirit still resisted." Kelgar lowered his head. "If only I had been as strong."

"You can be," said Thrall. "Come with me, Kelgar. I am strong, I can easily pull you up over the walls if—"

Kelgar shook his head. "It is not the strength that is gone, Thrall. I could kill the guards in a heartbeat. Anyone here could. It's the desire. I do not wish to try to climb the walls. I want to stay here. I can't explain it, and I am ashamed, but that is the truth. You will have to have the passion, the fire, for all of us here."

Thrall nodded his acceptance, though he could not understand. Who wouldn't want to be free? Who wouldn't want to fight, to gain back all that had been taken, to make the unjust humans pay for what they had done to his people? But it was clear: Of all of the orcs present, he was the only one who would dare lift a defiant fist in challenge.

He would wait until nightfall. Kelgar said there was only a skeleton roster of guardsmen, and they often drank themselves into a stupor. If Thrall simply continued to pretend he was like all the other orcs, he felt certain his opportunity would come.

At that moment, a female orc approached. She moved with a sense of purpose rarely seen here, and Thrall stood as it became clear that she was heading for him.

"You are the newly captured orc?" she asked, in human speech.

Thrall nodded. "My name is Thrall."

"Then, Thrall, you had best know that the commander of the encampments is coming for you."

"What is his name?" Thrall went cold inside as he feared the worst.

"I do not know, but he wears the colors red and gold, with a black falcon on—"

"Blackmoore," hissed Thrall. "I should have known he would be able to find me."

There was a loud clanging and all the orcs turned toward the large tower. "We are to line up," said the female. "Although it is not the usual time for counting."

"They want you, Thrall," said Kelgar. "But they won't find you. You will have to go now. The guards will be distracted at the thought of the commander coming. I will create a diversion. The least guarded area is at the end of the camp. We all are coming to the sound of the bell like the cattle we are," he said, self-loathing plain in his voice and mien. "Go. Now."

Thrall needed no further urging. He turned on his heel and began to move swiftly, threading his way between the sudden press of orcs moving in the opposite direction. As he shoved, struggling, he heard a cry of pain. It was the female orc. He didn't dare stop to look back, but when he heard Kelgar shouting harsh-sounding words in orcish, he understood. Kelgar had somehow managed to reach deep inside and find a shadow of his old fighting spirit. He had begun to fight with the female orc. By the sounds of the guards, this was highly unusual. They descended to break the quarreling orcs apart, and even as Thrall watched, the few guards who had been walking the wall scurried down and raced toward the shouting.

They would probably beat both Kelgar and the innocent female, Thrall thought. He regretted this deeply. But, he told himself, because of their actions, I am free to do everything I possibly can to ensure that no human ever, *ever* beats an orc again.

After having reached adulthood in a tightly guarded cell, with men watching his every move, he could not believe how easy it was to climb the walls and slip down to freedom. Ahead was a dense, forested area. He ran faster than he had ever run, knowing that every minute he was in the open he was vulnerable. And yet, no one cried the alarm, no one gave chase.

He ran for several hours, losing himself in the forest, zigging and zagging and doing everything possible to make it difficult for the search parties that would no doubt follow. Finally, he slowed, panting and gasping for air. He climbed a stout tree, and when he poked his head through its thick canopy of leaves, he could see nothing but a sea of green.

Blinking, he located the sun. It was starting its late afternoon journey toward the horizon. The west; Kelgar had said that Grom Hellscream's clan had come from the west.

He would find this Hellscream, and together, they would liberate their imprisoned brothers and sisters.

Black-gloved hands clasped behind him, the Commander of the Camps, one Aedelas Blackmoore, walked slowly down the line of orcs. All of them shied away from him, staring at their mud-encrusted feet. Blackmoore had to admit they had been more entertaining, if more deadly, when they had had some spirit to them.

Wincing at the stench, Blackmoore lifted a scented kerchief to his nose. Following him closely, like a dog awaiting its master's whim, was Major Remka. He'd heard good things about her; she was apparently more efficient than the majority of the men.

But if she had had his Thrall, and let him slip through her fingers, he would not be merciful.

"Where is the one you said you thought was Thrall?" he demanded of Remka's guardsman Waryk. The young man held his composure better than his commanding officer did, but even he was starting to show hints of panic about the eyes.

"I had seen him at the gladiator battles, and the blue

eyes are so rare. . . ." said Waryk, starting to stammer a little.

"Do you see him here?"

"N-no, Lieutenant General. I don't."

"Then perhaps it was not Thrall."

"We did find some things he had stolen," said Waryk, brightening. He snapped his fingers and one of his men raced off, returning in a few moments with a large sack. "Do you recognize this?" He extended a plain dagger to Blackmoore, hilt first as etiquette demanded.

Blackmoore's breath caught in his throat. He had wondered where that had gone to. It wasn't a very expensive one, but he had missed it. . . . He ran his gloved thumb over the symbol of his crest, the black falcon. "This is mine. Anything else?"

"Some papers . . . Major Remka has not had time to look at them yet. . . ." Waryk's voice trailed off, but Blackmoore understood. The idiot couldn't read. What kind of papers could Thrall possibly have had? Leaves torn from *his* books, no doubt. Blackmoore snatched the sack and rummaged through the papers at the bottom. He drew one out into the light.

> . . . *wish I could talk to you instead of just sending you these letters. I see you in the ring and my heart breaks for you.* . . .

Letters! Who could possibly . . . he seized another one.

*. . . harder and harder to find time to write. Our
Master demands so much of both of us. I heard that
he beat you, I am so sorry my dear friend. You don't
deserve . . .*

Taretha.

A greater pain than any he had ever known clutched
at Blackmoore's chest. He pulled out more letters . . .
by the Light, there had to be dozens here . . . maybe
hundreds. How long had the two been conspiring? For
some reason his eyes stung and breathing became difficult. *Tari . . . Tari, how could you, you never lacked for anything. . . .*

"My lord?" Remka's concerned voice brought
Blackmoore out of his painful shock. He took a deep
breath and blinked the telltale tears back. "Is all well?"

"No, Major Remka." His voice was as cool and composed as ever, for which he was grateful. "All is not
well. You had my orc Thrall, one of the finest gladiators ever to have graced the ring. He's made me a great
deal of money over the years and was supposed to
make me a great deal more. Beyond a doubt, it was he
your man captured. And it is he whom I do not see in
this line at all."

He took keen pleasure in watching the color drain
from Remka's face. "He could be hiding inside the
camp," she offered.

"He could be," said Blackmoore, drawing back his
lips from white teeth in a rictus of a smile. "Let us hope

so, for your continued good fortune, Major Remka. Search the encampment. *Now.*"

She scurried away to do his bidding, shouting orders. Thrall certainly wouldn't have been stupid enough to come to a lineup, like a dog responding to a whistle. It was possible he was still here. But somehow, Blackmoore sensed that Thrall was gone. He was elsewhere, doing . . . ? What? What kind of scheme had he and that bitch Taretha cooked up?

Blackmoore was right. An extensive search turned up nothing. None of the orcs, curse them, would even admit to seeing Thrall. Blackmoore demoted Remka, put Waryk in her place, and rode slowly home. Langston met him halfway, and commiserated with him, but even Langston's cheerful, brainless chatter could not stir Blackmoore from his gloom. In one fiery night, he had lost the two things most important to him: Thrall and Taretha.

He climbed the steps to his quarters, went to his bedchamber, and eased open the door. The light fell across Taretha's sleeping face. Gently, so as not to wake her, Blackmoore sat down on the bed. He removed his gloves and reached to touch the soft, creamy curve of her cheek. She was so beautiful. Her touch had thrilled him, her laughter moved him. But no more.

"Sleep well, pretty traitor," he whispered. He bent and kissed her, the pain in his heart still present but ruthlessly suppressed. "Sleep well, until I have need of you."

NINE

Thrall had never been so exhausted or hungry in his life. But freedom tasted sweeter than the meat he had been fed, and felt more restful than the straw upon which he had slept as Blackmoore's prisoner at Durnholde. He was unable to catch the coneys and squirrels that flitted through the forest, and wished that somehow survival skills had been taught to him along with battle histories and the nature of art. Because it was autumn, there were ripe fruits on the trees, and he quickly became adept at finding grubs and insects. These did little to appease the mammoth hunger that gnawed at his insides, but at least he had ready access to water in the form of the myriad small streams and brooks that wound through the forest.

After several days, the wind shifted while Thrall

steadily pushed through the undergrowth and brought the sweet scent of roasting meat to his nostrils. He inhaled deeply, as if he could obtain sustenance by the smell alone. Ravenous, he turned to follow the smell.

Even though his body was crying out for food, Thrall did not let his hunger overcome his caution. That was well, for as he moved to the edge of the forested area, he saw dozens of humans.

The day was bright and warm, one of the last few such days of the fall, and the humans were joyfully preparing a feast that made Thrall's mouth water. There were baked breads, barrels of fresh fruits and vegetables, crocks of jams and butters and spreads, wheels of cheeses, bottles of what he assumed were wine and mead, and in the center, two pigs turned slowly on spits.

Thrall's knees gave way and he sank slowly to the forest floor, staring enraptured at the foodstuffs spread before him as if to taunt him. Over in the cleared field, children played with hoops and banners and other toys Thrall could not attach names to. Mothers suckled their babes, and maidens danced shyly with young men. It was a scene of happiness and contentment, and more than the food, Thrall wanted to belong here.

But he did not. He was an orc, a monster, a greenskin, a black-blood, and any of a hundred other epithets. So he sat and watched while the villagers celebrated, feasted, and danced until the night encroached upon them.

The moons rose, one bright and white, one cool and blue-green, as the last of the furniture, plates, and food items were gathered up. Thrall watched the villagers wander down the winding path through the field, and saw small candles appear in tiny windows. Still he waited, and watched the moons move slowly across the sky. Many hours after the last candle was extinguished in the windows, Thrall rose, and moved with skillful silence toward the village.

His sense of smell had always been acute, and it was sharpened now that he was giving it leave to enjoy the smells of food. He followed the scents, reaching into windows and snatching whole loaves of bread which he gobbled down at once, uncovering a basket of apples set out by the door and crunching the small, sweet fruits greedily.

Juice ran down his bare chest, sweet and sticky. He absently wiped at it with one large green hand. Slowly, the hunger was beginning to be sated. At each house, Thrall took something, but never too much from any one home.

At one window, Thrall peered in to see figures sleeping by the dying hearth fire. He quickly withdrew, waited a moment, and then slowly looked in again. These were children, sleeping on straw mattresses. There was three of them, plus one in a cradle. Two were boys; the third was a little girl with yellow hair. As Thrall watched, she rolled over in her sleep.

A sharp pang stabbed Thrall. As if no time at all had passed, he was transported in his mind back to that day when he had first seen Taretha, when she had smiled broadly and waved at him. This girl looked so much like her, with her round cheeks, her golden hair—

A harsh noise startled him and Thrall whirled just in time to see something four-legged and dark charge at him. Teeth snapped near his ear. Reacting instinctively, Thrall clutched the animal and closed his hands around the beast's throat. Was this a wolf, one of the creatures his people sometimes befriended?

It had erect, pointed ears, a long muzzle, and sharp white teeth. It resembled the woodcuts of wolves he had seen in the books, but was very different in coloring and head shape.

Now the house was awake, and he heard human voices crying in alarm. He squeezed, and the creature went limp. Dropping the body, Thrall looked inside to see the little girl staring at him with eyes wide in horror. As he watched, she screamed and pointed. "Monster, Da, monster!"

The hateful words coming from her innocent lips wounded Thrall to the quick. He turned to flee only to see that a ring of frightened villagers surrounded him. Some of them carried pitchforks and scythes, the only weapons this farming community possessed.

"I mean you no harm," Thrall began.

"It talks! It's a demon!" screamed someone, and the little band charged.

Thrall reacted instinctively and his training kicked in. When one of the men shoved a pitchfork at him, Thrall deftly seized the makeshift weapon and used it to knock the other forks and scythes out of the clumsy villagers' hands. At one point he screamed his battle cry, the bloodlust high within him, and swung the pitchfork at his attackers.

He stopped just short of impaling the fallen man, who stared up at him wildly.

These men were not his enemies, even though it was clear they feared and hated him. They were simple farmers, living off the crops they grew and the animals they raised. They had children. They were afraid of him, that was all. No, the enemy was not here. The enemy was sleeping soundly on a featherbed in Durnholde. With a cry of self-loathing, Thrall hurled the pitchfork several yards away and took advantage of the break in the circle to flee for the safety of the forest.

The men did not pursue. Thrall had not expected them to. They only wished to be left in peace. As he ran through the forest, utilizing the energy engendered by the confrontation to his advantage, Thrall tried, and failed, to erase the image of a little blond girl screaming in terror and calling him "monster."

Thrall ran through the next day and into the night, when he finally collapsed in exhaustion. He slept the sleep of the dead, with no dreams to plague him. Something roused him before the dawn, and he blinked sleepily.

There came a second sharp prod to the belly, and now he was fully awake—and staring up at eight angry orc faces.

He tried to rise, but they fell upon him and bound him before he could even struggle. One of them shoved a large, angry face with yellowed tusks within an inch of Thrall's. He barked something completely unintelligible, and Thrall shook his head.

The orc frowned even more terribly, grabbed one of Thrall's ears and uttered more gibberish.

Guessing at what the other might be saying, Thrall said in the human tongue, "No, I'm not deaf."

An angry hiss came from all of them. "Hu-man," said the big orc, who seemed to be their leader. "You not speak orcish?"

"A little," Thrall said in that language. "My name is Thrall."

The orc gaped, then opened his mouth and guffawed. His cronies joined him. "Hu-man who looks like an orc!" he said, extending a black-nailed finger in Thrall's direction. In orcish, he said, "Kill him."

"No!" Thrall cried in orcish. One thing about this fairly dire encounter gave him hope—these orcs were fighters. They did not slouch about in exhausted despair, too dispirited to even climb an easily scalable stone wall. "Want find Grom Hellscream!"

The big orc froze. In broken human, he said, "Why find? You sent to kill, huh? From human, huh?"

Thrall shook his head. "No. Camps . . . bad. Orcs. . . ." He couldn't find the words in this alien tongue, so he sighed deeply and hung his head, trying to look like the pitiable creatures he had met in the internment camp. "Me want orcs. . . ." He lifted his roped hands and bellowed. "Grom help. No more camps. No more orcs. . . ." Again, he mimed looking despondent and hopeless.

He risked a look up, wondering if his broken orcish had managed to convey what he wanted. At least they weren't trying to kill him anymore. Another orc, slightly smaller but equally as dangerous-looking as the first, spoke in a gruff voice. The leader responded heatedly. They argued back and forth, and then finally the big one seemed to give in.

"Tragg say, maybe. Maybe you see Hellscream, if you worthy. Come." They hauled him to his feet and marched him forward. The prod of the spear in his back encouraged Thrall to pick up the pace. Even though he was bound and at the center of a ring of hostile orcs, Thrall felt a surge of joy.

He was going to see Grom Hellscream, the one orc that remained uncowed. Perhaps together, they could free the imprisoned orcs, rouse them into action, and remind them of their birthrights.

While it was difficult for Thrall to summon many words of orc speech, he was able to understand much more than he could articulate. He remained quiet, and listened.

The orcs escorting him to see Hellscream were surprised by his vigor. Thrall had noticed that most of them had brown or black eyes, not the peculiar, burning red of most of the orcs in the internment camps. Kelgar had indicated that there might be some kind of connection between the glowing, fiery orbs and the peculiar lethargy that had all but overcome the orcs. What it was, Thrall didn't know, and by listening, he hoped to learn.

While the orcs said nothing of glowing red eyes, they did comment on the listlessness. Many of the words that Thrall did not understand were nonetheless comprehensible because of the tone of contempt in which they were uttered. Thrall was not alone in his revulsion and disgust at seeing the once-legendary fighting force brought lower than common cattle. At least a bull would charge you if you irritated it.

Of their great warlord, they spoke words of praise and awe. They also spoke of Thrall, wondering if he was some sort of new spy sent to discover Grom's lair and lead the humans to a cowardly ambush. Thrall desperately wished there were some way to convince them of his sincerity. He would do anything they wanted of him to prove himself.

At one point, the group came to a halt. The leader, whom Thrall had learned was named Rekshak, untied a sash from around his broad chest. He held it in both hands and went to Thrall. "You be. . . ." He said something in orcish that Thrall didn't understand, but he knew what Rekshak wanted. He lowered his head obediently, for he towered over all the other orcs, and permitted himself to be blindfolded. The sash smelled of new sweat and old blood.

Certainly, they might kill him now, or abandon him to die, bound and blindfolded. Thrall accepted that possibility and thought it preferable to another day spent risking his life in the gladiator pit for the glory of the cruel bastard who had beaten him and tried to break Tari's spirit.

Now he strode with less certain steps, though at one point two orcs silently went to either side of him and grasped his arms. He trusted them; he had no choice.

With no way to gauge the passing of time, the journey seemed to take forever. At one point the soft, springy forest loam gave way to chill stone, and the air around Thrall turned colder. By the way the other orcs' voices were altered, Thrall realized they were descending into the earth.

At last, they came to a halt. Thrall bowed his head and the sash was removed. Even the dim lighting provided by torches made him blink as his eyes adjusted from the utter darkness of the blindfold.

He was in an enormous underground cavern. Sharp stones thrust from both stone ceiling and floor. Thrall could hear the drip of moisture in the distance. There were several smaller caves leading out from this one large cavern, many with animal skins draped over the entrances. Armor that had seen better days, and weapons that looked well used and well cared for were scattered here and there. A small fire burned in the center, its smoke wafting up to the stone roof. This, then, must be where the legendary Grom Hellscream and the remnants of the once-fierce Warsong clan had retreated.

But where was the famous chieftain? Thrall looked around. While several more orcs had emerged from various caves, none had the bearing or garb of a true chieftain. He turned to Rekshak.

"You said you would take me to Hellscream," he demanded. "I do not see him here."

"You do not see him, but he is present. He sees you," said another orc, brushing aside an animal skin and emerging into the cavern. This one was almost as tall as Thrall, but without the bulk. He looked older, and very tired. The bones of various animals and quite possibly humans were strung on a necklace about his thin throat. He carried himself in a manner that demanded respect, and Thrall was willing to give it. Whoever this orc was, he was a personage of importance in the clan. And it was clear he spoke the human tongue almost as fluently as Thrall

Thrall inclined his head. "This may be. But I wish to speak with him, not merely bask in his unseen presence."

The orc smiled. "You have spirit, fire," he said. "That is well. I am Iskar, adviser to the great chieftain Hellscream."

"My name is—"

"You are not unknown to us, Thrall of Durnholde." At Thrall's look of surprise, Iskar continued, "Many have heard of Lieutenant General Blackmoore's pet orc."

Thrall growled, softly, deep in his throat, but he did not lose his composure. He had heard the term before, but it rankled more coming from the mouth of one of his own people.

"We have never seen you fight, of course," Iskar continued, clasping his hands behind his back and walking a slow circle around Thrall, looking him up and down all the while. "Orcs aren't allowed to watch the gladiator battles. While you were finding glory in the ring, your brethren were beaten and abused."

Thrall could take it no longer. "I received none of the glory. I was a slave, owned by Blackmoore, and if you do not think I despise him, look at this!" He twisted around so that they could see his back. They looked, and then to his fury they laughed.

"There is nothing to see, Thrall of Durnholde," Iskar said. Thrall realized what had happened; the healing salve had worked its magic all too well. There was not even a scar on his back from the terrible beating he had received from Blackmoore and all of his men. "You ask for our compassion, and yet you seem hale and healthy to us."

Thrall whirled. Anger filled him, and he tried to temper it, but to little avail. "I was a thing, a piece of property. Do you think I benefited from my sweat and blood shed in the ring? Blackmoore hauled in gold coins while I was kept in a cell, brought out for his amusement. The scars on my body are not visible, I realize that now. But the only reason I was healed was so that I could go back in the ring and fight again to enrich my master. There are scars you cannot see that run much deeper. I escaped, I was thrown into the camps, and then I came here to find Hellscream. Although I begin to doubt his existence. It seems too much to hope for that I could still find an orc who exemplifies all that I understood our people to be."

"What do you understand our people to be, then, orc who bears the name of slave?" Iskar taunted.

Thrall was breathing heavily, but summoned the control that Sergeant had taught him. "They are strong. Cunning. Powerful. They are a terror in battle. They have spirits that cannot be quenched. Let me see Hellscream, and he will know that I am worthy."

"We will be the judge of that," said Iskar. He raised his hand, and three orcs entered the cavern. They began to don armor and reach for various weapons. "These three are our finest warriors. They are, as you have said, strong, cunning, and powerful. They fight to kill or die, unlike what you are used to in the gladiator ring. Your playacting will not serve you here. Only real skill will save you. If you survive, Hellscream may grant you an audience, or he may not."

Thrall gazed at Iskar. "He will see me," he said confidently.

"You had best hope so. Begin!" And with no further warning, all three orcs charged at a weaponless, armorless Thrall.

TEN

For the briefest of moments, Thrall was caught off guard. Then years of training took over. While he had no desire to fight his own people, he was able to quickly regard them as combatants in the ring and react accordingly. As one of them charged, Thrall swiftly dodged and then reached upward, snatching the huge battle-ax from the orc's hands. In the same fluid motion, he swung. The blow bit deeply, but the armor deflected most of the strike. The orc cried out and stumbled to his feet, clutching his back. He would survive, but that quickly, the odds had been reduced to two to one.

Thrall whirled, snarling. The bloodlust, sweet and familiar, filled him again. Bellowing his own challenge, a second adversary charged, wielding an enormous broadsword that more than compensated for his lack of arm length. Thrall twisted to the side, avoiding a killing blow but still feeling the hot pain as the blade bit into his side.

The orc pressed his attack, and at the same time, the third orc came in from behind. Thrall, though, now had a weapon. He ignored the blood pumping from his side, making the stone floor slick and treacherous, and swung the huge ax first toward one attacker, then letting the momentum swing it back to strike the second.

They parried with enormous shields. Thrall had no armor or shielding, but fighting this way was something he was used to. These were clever opponents, but so had the human fighters been. They were strong and physically powerful, but so were the trolls Thrall had faced and defeated. He moved from a place of calm surety, dodging and screaming and striking. Once, they might have been a threat to him. Now, though, even at two to one, as long as Thrall was able to keep his eye on strategy and not succumb to the sweet call of bloodlust, he knew he would triumph.

His arm moved as if of its own accord, striking blow after blow. Even when his feet slipped and he fell, he used it to his advantage. He angled his body so it would strike one opponent, while extending his arm to its full length so that the huge ax would swipe the other orc's legs out from under him. He was careful to angle the ax so that the blunt end struck, not the blade. He did not wish to kill these orcs; he only wished to win the fight.

Both orcs went down hard. The orc Thrall had struck with the ax clutched his legs and howled his frustration. It appeared they had both been broken. The other orc staggered to his feet and tried to impale Thrall with the broadsword.

Thrall made his decision. Steeling himself for the pain, he reached upward with both hands, grasped the blade, and yanked it forward. The orc lost his balance and fell atop Thrall's body. Thrall twisted and in a heartbeat found himself straddling the other orc, his hands at his throat.

Squeeze, instinct cried. *Squeeze tight. Kill Blackmoore for what he did to you.*

No! he thought. This was not Blackmoore. This was one of his people, whom he had risked everything to find. He rose and extended a hand to the defeated orc to help him up.

The orc stared at the hand. "We kill," said Iskar, his voice as calm as before. "Kill your opponent, Thrall. It's what a real orc would do."

Thrall shook his head slowly, reached down to clasp his opponent's arm, and hauled the vanquished foe to his feet. "In battle, yes. I would kill my foe in battle, so that he did not rise up against me at another time. But you are my people, whether you will own me as one of you or not. We are too few in number for me to kill him."

Iskar looked at him strangely, seemed to be waiting for something, then continued speaking.

"Your reasoning is understandable. You have honorably defeated our three finest warriors. You have passed the first test."

First? Thrall thought, one hand going to his bleeding side. A suspicion began to form that no matter how many "tests" he passed, they would not let him see Hellscream. Perhaps Hellscream was not even here.

Perhaps Hellscream was no longer even *alive*.

But Thrall knew in his heart of hearts that even if this were so, he would rather die here than return to his life under Blackmoore's boot.

"What is the next challenge?" he asked quietly. He could tell by the reaction that his calm demeanor impressed them.

"A question of will," said Iskar. There was a slight smirk on his heavy-jawed face. He gestured, and an orc emerged from one of the caves carrying what appeared at first glance to be a heavy sack on his back. But when he carelessly tossed the "sack" onto the stone floor, Thrall realized that it was a male human child, bound hand and foot and with a gag thrust into his mouth. The child's black hair was tangled. He was filthy, and where dirt did not cover his pale flesh, Thrall saw the purple and green of bruises. His eyes were the same color as Thrall's own, a rich blue, and those eyes were wide with terror.

"You know what this is," said Iskar.

"A child. A human child," Thrall replied, perplexed. Surely they did not expect him to fight the boy.

"A male child. Males mature to become orc-killers. They are our natural enemies. If you indeed chafed at the whip and rod, and wish for revenge on those who enslaved you and even gave you a name to mark your low position in life, then exact your revenge now. Kill this child, before he grows to be of an age to kill you."

The boy's eyes widened, for Iskar had been speaking in the human tongue. He squirmed frantically and muffled sounds came from his mouth. The orc who had carried him out kicked him disinterestedly in the stomach. The child curled up tightly, whimpering past the gag.

Thrall stared. Surely they were not serious. He looked over at Iskar, who regarded him without blinking.

"This is no warrior," said Thrall. "And this is no honorable combat. I had thought that orcs prized their honor."

"So we do," agreed Iskar, "but before you lies a future threat. Defend your people."

"He is a child!" Thrall exclaimed. "He is no threat now, and who can say what he will be? I know the clothes he wears, and what village he was taken from. The people there are farmers and herders. They live on what they raise, both fruit and flesh. Their weapons are for hunting coneys and deer, not orcs."

"But there is a good chance that, if we again go to war, this boy will be in the front line, charging at one of us with a spear and calling for our blood," Iskar retorted. "Do you wish to see Hellscream or not? If you do not slay the child, you may rest assured that you will not leave this cave alive."

The boy was crying now, silently. Thrall was instantly reminded of his parting with Taretha, and her description of weeping. Her image filled his mind. He thought of her, and of Sergeant. He thought of how

saddened he had been when his appearance had frightened the little girl in the village.

And then he thought of Blackmoore's handsome,
contemptuous face; of all the men who had spat upon
him and called him "monster" and "greenskin" and
worse.

But those memories did not condone cold-blooded
murder. Thrall made his decision. He dropped the
bloody ax to the floor.

"If this child takes up arms against me in the future,"
he said, choosing his words slowly and deliberately,
"then I shall kill him on the battlefield. And I shall take
a certain pleasure in the doing, because I will know that
I am fighting for the rights of my people. But I will not
kill a bound child who lies helpless before me, human
though he is. And if this means I never see Hellscream,
so be it. If it means I must fight all of you and fall beneath your numbers, I say again, so be it. I would rather
die than commit such a dishonorable atrocity."

He steadied himself, arms outstretched, waiting for
the attack that would come. Iskar sighed.

"A pity," he said, "but you have chosen your own
destiny." He lifted his hand.

At that moment, a terrible scream pierced the still,
cool air. It echoed and reverberated through the cavern, hurting Thrall's ears and piercing him to the bone.
He shrank back from the noise. The animal skin covering one of the caves was torn down and a tall, red-eyed
orc emerged. Thrall had gotten used to the appearance

of his people, but this orc was unlike any he had yet seen.

Long black hair flowed down his back in a thick tangle. Each large ear was pierced several times, reminding Thrall oddly of Sergeant, and the dozen or so rings glinted in the firelight. His leather clothing of red and black contrasted strikingly with his green skin, and several chains attached to various places on his body swayed with his movements. His entire jaw seemed to be painted black, and at the moment, it was open wider than Thrall would have believed possible. It was he who was making the terrifying noise, and Thrall realized that Grom Hellscream had gotten his name for a very good reason.

The shriek faded, and Grom spoke. "Never had I thought to see this!" He marched up to Thrall and stared at him. His eyes were flame-colored, and something dark and frightening seemed to dance in their centers in place of pupils. Thrall assumed the comment to be derogatory, but he was not about to be cowed. He drew himself up to his full imposing height, determined to meet death with an unbowed head. He opened his mouth to reply to Grom's comment, but the orc chieftain continued.

"How is it you know of mercy, Thrall of Durnholde? How is it you know when to offer it, and for what reasons?"

The orcs were murmuring among themselves now, confused. Iskar bowed.

"Noble Hellscream," he began, "we had thought

that this child's capture would please you. We expected—"

"*I* would expect that its parents would track it down to our lair, you fool!" cried Grom. "We are warriors, fierce and proud. At least we once were." He shuddered, as if from a fever, and for a moment seemed to Thrall to be pale and tired. But that impression was gone as quickly as it had come. "We do not butcher children. I assume whoever caught the whelp had the presence of mind to blindfold it?"

"Of course, lord," said Rekshak, looking offended.

"Then take him back where you found him the same way." Hellscream marched over to the child and removed the gag. The boy was too terrified to cry out. "Listen to me, tiny human. Tell your people that the orcs had you, and chose not to harm you. Tell them," and he looked over at Thrall, "that they showed you mercy. Also tell them if they try to find us, they will fail. We will be on the move soon. Do you understand?"

The boy nodded. "Good." To Rekshak, he said, "Take him back. *Now*. And the next time you find a human pup, leave it be."

Rekshak nodded. With a definite lack of gentleness, he took the boy by the arm and hauled him to his feet.

"Rekshak," said Grom, his harsh voice heavy with warning. "If you disobey me and the boy comes to harm, I shall know of it. And I shall not forgive."

Rekshak scowled impotently. "As my lord wills," he said, and, still roughly hauling the boy, began to ascend one of the many winding stone corridors that emptied into the cavern.

Iskar looked confused. "My lord," he began, "this is the pet of Blackmoore! He stinks of humans, he brags of his fear of killing—"

"I have no fear of killing those who deserve to die," Thrall growled. "I do not choose to kill those who do not."

Hellscream reached out and put a hand on Iskar's shoulder, then placed the other on Thrall's, reaching up to do so. "Iskar, my old friend," he said, his rough voice soft, "you have seen me when the bloodlust has come upon me. You have seen me wade in blood up to my knees. I have killed the children of the humans ere now. But we gave all we had fighting in that manner, and where has it brought us? Low and defeated, our kind slouch in camps and lift no hand to free themselves, let alone fight for others. That way of fighting, of making war, has brought us to this. Long have I thought that the ancestors would show me a new way, a way to win back what we have lost. It is a fool who repeats the same actions expecting a different outcome, and whatever I may be, I am not a fool. Thrall was strong enough to defeat the finest we had to offer. He has tasted humankind's ways and turned his back on them to be free. He has escaped from the camps and against the odds managed to find me. I agree with his choices here today. One day, my old friend, you, too, will see the wisdom in this."

He squeezed Iskar's shoulder affectionately. "Leave us, now. All of you."

Slowly, reluctantly, and not without a few hostile glances in Thrall's direction, the orcs all ascended into different levels of the cave. Thrall waited.

"We are alone now," said Hellscream. "Are you hungry, Thrall of Durnholde?"

"I am ravenous," said Thrall, "but I would ask that you not call me Thrall of Durnholde. I escaped Durnholde, and I loathe the thought of it."

Hellscream lumbered over to another cave, pulled the skin aside, and withdrew a large chunk of raw meat. Thrall accepted it, nodded his thanks, and bit into it eagerly. His first honestly earned meal as a free orc. Deer flesh had never tasted so fine to him.

"Should we then change your other name? It is the term of a slave," said Hellscream, squatting and watching Thrall closely with red eyes. "It was meant to be a badge of shame."

Thrall thought as he chewed and swallowed. "No. Blackmoore gave me the name so that I would never forget that I was something he owned, that I belonged to him." His eyes narrowed. "I never will. I will keep the name, and one day, when I see him again, he will be the one who remembers what he did to me, and regret it with all his heart."

Hellscream regarded him closely. "You would kill him, then?"

Thrall did not answer immediately. He thought of

the time when he had almost killed Sergeant and seen Blackmoore's face instead, of the countless times since that moment when he had visualized Blackmoore's handsome, taunting visage while fighting in the ring. He thought of Blackmoore's slurred speech and the agony that his kicks and fists had caused. He thought of the anguish on Taretha's lovely face as she spoke of the master of Durnholde.

"Yes," he said, his voice deep and hard. "I would. If any creature deserves death, it is certainly Aedelas Blackmoore."

Hellscream cackled, a strange, wild sound. "Good. At least you're willing to kill somebody. I was starting to wonder if I'd made the right choice." He gestured to the tattered cloth that Thrall had tucked into the waistband of his trousers. "That doesn't look human-made."

Thrall tugged the swaddling cloth free. "It isn't. This is the cloth in which Blackmoore found me, when I was an infant." He handed it to Hellscream. "That's all I know."

"I know this pattern," said Hellscream, opening the cloth and regarding the symbol of the white wolf's head on a blue background. "This is the symbol of the Frostwolf clan. Where did Blackmoore find you?"

"He always told me it wasn't very far from Durnholde," said Thrall.

"Then your family was a long way from home. I wonder why."

Hope seized Thrall. "Did you know them? Could

you tell me who my parents were? There is so much I don't know."

"I can only say that this is the emblem of the Frostwolf clan, and that they live a great distance from here, somewhere up in the mountains. They were exiled by Gul'dan. I never did learn why. Durotan and his people seemed loyal to me. Rumor has it they have formed bonds with the wild white wolves, but one cannot always believe everything that one hears."

Thrall tasted disappointment. Still, it was more than he had known before. He ran a big hand over the small square of old fabric, amazed that he had ever been little enough to be wrapped in it.

"Another question, if you can answer it," he said to Hellscream. "When I was younger, I was training outside, and a wagon passed, carrying several. . . ." He paused. What was the correct term? Inmates? Slaves? "Several orcs to the internment camps. One of them broke free and attacked me. He kept screaming something over and over. I was never able to learn what he said, but I vowed I would remember the words. Perhaps you can tell me what they mean."

"Speak, and I shall tell you."

"Kagh! Bin mog g'thazag cha!" said Thrall.

"That was no attack, my young friend," said Hellscream. "The words are, 'Run! I will protect you!' "

Thrall stared. All this time, he had assumed that he was the object of the charge, when all along. . . .

"The other fighters," he said. "We were doing a

training exercise. I was without armor or shield, in the center of a ring of men. . . . He died, Hellscream. They cut him to bits. He thought they were making sport of me, that I was being attacked twelve to one. He died to protect me."

Hellscream said nothing, merely continued to eat while watching Thrall closely. Famished though he was, Thrall let the haunch of meat drip its juices onto the stone floor. Someone had given his life to protect an unknown young orc. Slowly, without the keen pleasure he had experienced before, he bit into the flesh and chewed. Sooner or later, he would have to find the Frostwolf clan, and learn exactly who he was.

ELEVEN

Thrall had never known such joy. For the next several days, he feasted with the Warsong clan, sang their fierce battle chants and songs, and learned at Hellscream's feet.

Far from being the mindless killing machines the books had painted them, Thrall learned that the orcs were of a noble race. They were masters on the battlefield, and had been known to revel in the spray of blood and the crack of bone, but their culture was a rich, elaborate one. Hellscream spoke of a time when each clan was separate unto itself. Each had its own symbols, customs, even speech. There were spiritual leaders among them, called shamans, who worked with the magic of nature and not the evil magic of demonic, supernatural powers.

"Isn't magic magic?" Thrall, who had very little experience with magic in any form, wanted to know.

"Yes and no," said Grom. "Sometimes the effect is the same. For instance, if a shaman was to summon lightning to strike his foes, they would be burned to death. If a warlock was to summon hell's flames against an enemy, they would be burned to death."

"So magic is magic," said Thrall.

"But," Grom continued, "lightning is a natural phenomenon. You call it by requesting it. With hell's fire, you make a bargain. It costs a little of yourself."

"But you said that the shamans were disappearing. Doesn't that mean that the warlock's way was better?"

"The warlock's way was quicker," said Grom. "More effective, or so it seemed. But there comes a time when a price must be paid, and sometimes, it is dear indeed."

Thrall learned that he was not the only one appalled by the peculiar lethargy demonstrated by the vast majority of orcs, now languishing apathetically in the internment camps.

"No one can explain it," said Hellscream, "but it claimed nearly all of us, one by one. We thought it some kind of illness at first, but it does not kill and it does not worsen after a certain point."

"One of the orcs in the camp thought it had something to do with—" Thrall fell silent, having no desire to give offense.

"Speak!" demanded Grom, annoyed. "To do with what?"

"With the redness of the eyes," said Thrall.

"Ah," said Grom, with, Thrall thought, a trace of

sorrow. "Perhaps it does, at that. There is something we wrestle with that you, blue-eyed youngling, cannot understand. I hope you never do." And for the second time since Thrall had met him, Hellscream appeared to him to be small and frail. He was thin, Thrall realized; it was his ferocity, his battle cry, which made him appear to be so threatening and powerful. Physically, the charismatic leader of the Warsongs was wasting away. Even though he barely knew Hellscream, the realization moved Thrall. It seemed as though the orc chieftain's will and powerful personality was the only thing keeping him alive, that he was bone and blood and sinew tied together by the barest of threads.

He did not voice his perception; Grom Hellscream knew it. Their eyes met. Hellscream nodded, and then changed the subject.

"They have nothing to hope for, nothing to fight for," Hellscream said. "You told me that one orc was able to rally enough to fight with a friend in order to provide a way for you to escape. That gives me hope. If these people thought that there was some way they could matter, take their destinies into their own hands—I believe they would rouse themselves. None of us has ever been in one of these accursed camps. Tell us all you know, Thrall."

Thrall willingly obliged, pleased to be of some help. He described the camp, the orcs, the guards, and the security measures in as much detail as he could. Hellscream listened intently, now and then interrupting with a question or asking him to elaborate. When

Thrall was finished, Hellscream was silent for a moment.

"It is well," he said at last. "The humans are lulled into a sense of safety by our shameful lack of honor. We can use this to our advantage. It has long been a dream of mine, Thrall, to storm these wretched places and liberate the orcs held captive there. Yet I fear that once the gate is down, like the cattle they seem to have become, they will not fly to freedom."

"Regrettably, that seems true," said Thrall.

Grom swore colorfully. "It is up to us to awaken them from their strange dreams of despair and defeat. I think it no accident, Thrall, that you have come at this time. Gul'dan is no more, and his warlocks are scattered. It is time for what we once were to reemerge." His crimson eyes glittered. "And you will be part of that."

There was no relief for Blackmoore any longer.

With each day that crept by, he knew there was less and less a chance that Thrall would be located. They had been probably only moments behind him at the internment camp, and the incident had left a bitter taste in his mouth.

Which he tried to wash away with beer, mead, and wine.

After that, nothing. Thrall had seemingly vanished, a difficult task for something as big and ugly as an orc. Sometimes, when the empty bottles began to pile up beside him, Blackmoore was convinced that everyone was conspiring against him to keep Thrall away. This theory was lent credence by the fact that at least one person close to him had most certainly betrayed him. He held her close at night, lest she suspect he knew; enjoyed her physically, perhaps with more roughness than usual; spoke fairly to her. And yet sometimes, when she slept, the pain and anger were so overwhelming that he crawled out of the bed they shared and drank himself into a stupor.

And of course, with Thrall gone, all hope of leading an orcish army against the Alliance had disappeared like morning mist under a harsh sun. What then would become of Aedelas Blackmoore? Bad enough that he had to overcome the stigma of his father's name and prove himself a dozen times over, whereas lesser men were accepted at face value. They had told him, of course, that his present position was an honor, one he had richly earned. But he was far from the seat of power, and out of sight meant out of mind. Who in any real position of power thought of Blackmoore? No one, that was who, and it was making Blackmoore sick to his stomach.

He took another long, thirsty drink. A cautious tap came on his door. "Go away," he snarled.

"My lord?" The tentative voice of the betraying whore's rabbit of a father. "There is news, my lord. Lord Langston is here to see you."

Hope surged through Blackmoore and he struggled to rise from the bed. It was midafternoon and Taretha was off doing whatever it was she did when she wasn't serving him. He swung his booted feet to the floor and sat there a moment while the world swirled about him. "Send him in, Tammis," he ordered.

The door opened and Langston entered. "Wonderful news, my lord!" he exclaimed. "We have had a sighting of Thrall."

Blackmoore sniffed. "Sightings" of Thrall had become quite commonplace, considering there was a substantial reward offered. But Langston wouldn't come rushing to Blackmoore with unverified rumors. "Who saw him? Where?"

"Several leagues from the internment camp, headed due west," said Langston. "Several villagers were awakened when an orc tried to break into their homes. Seems it was hungry. When they surrounded it, it spoke fair to them, and when they pressed their attack, it fought back and overcame them."

"Anyone killed?" Blackmoore hoped not. He would have to pay the village if his pet had killed someone.

"No. In fact, they said the orc deliberately refrained from killing. A few days later, one of the farmer's sons was kidnapped by a group of orcs. He was taken to a subterranean cavern and they ordered a large orc to kill him. The orc refused, and the orc chieftain agreed with the decision. The boy was released and immediately told his story. And my lord—the confrontation took place with the orcs speaking in the human tongue, because the large orc could not understand the language of his fellows."

Blackmoore nodded. It all rang true with what he knew Thrall to be, versus what the populace assumed Thrall would be. Plus, a young boy wouldn't likely be clever enough to realize that Thrall didn't know much orcish.

By the Light . . . maybe they would find him.

There had been another rumor as to Thrall's whereabouts, and once again, Blackmoore had left Durnholde to follow up on it. Taretha had two passionate, conflicting thoughts. One was that she desperately hoped that the rumors were false, that Thrall was miles away from wherever it was he had been reportedly seen. The other was the overwhelming sense of relief she experienced whenever Blackmoore was not present.

She took her daily stroll around the grounds outside the fortress. It was safe these days, save for the occasional highwayman, and they skulked by the main roads. She would come to no harm in the forests that she had grown to know so intimately.

She undid her hair and let it cascade about her shoulders, enjoying the freedom of it. It was not seemly for a woman to have unbound hair. Gleefully, Taretha combed her fingers through the thick golden mass and shook her head in defiance.

Her gaze fell to the welts on her wrists. Instinctively, one hand reached to cover the other.

No. She would not hide what was not her own shame. Taretha forced herself to uncover the bruises.

For the sake of her family, she had to submit to him. But she would not aid in hiding the wrongs he had done.

Taretha took a deep breath. Even here, it would seem, Blackmoore's shadow followed. Deliberately, she banished it, and turned her face up toward the sun.

She wandered up to the cave where she had said her farewells to Thrall and sat there for a while, hugging her long legs to her chest. There was no sign that anyone save the creatures of the woods had been here in a long time. She then rose and strolled to the tree where she had told Thrall to hide the necklace she'd given him. Peering down into its blackened depths, she saw no glint of silver. She was relieved and saddened at the same time. Taretha desperately missed writing to Thrall and hearing his kind, wise replies.

If only the rest of her people felt that way. Couldn't they see that the orcs were not a threat anymore? Couldn't they understand that with education and a little bit of respect, they could be valuable allies and not enemies? She thought of all the money and time being poured into the internment camps, of how foolish and small-minded it seemed.

Too bad she couldn't have run away with Thrall. As Taretha walked slowly back to the fortress, she heard a horn blow. The master of Durnholde had returned. All the sense of lightness and freedom she had experienced bled out of her, as if from an open wound.

Whatever betide, Thrall at least is free, she thought. *My days as a slave loom numberless ahead of me.*

Thrall fought, and ate food prepared in the traditional way, and learned. Soon he was speaking fluent, if heavily accented, orcish. He could go with the hunting parties and be more of a help than a hindrance in bringing down a stag. Fingers that, despite their thickness, had learned to master a stylus had no difficulty helping build snares for rabbits and other smaller animals. Bit by bit, the Warsong clan was accepting him. For the first time in his life, Thrall felt as though he belonged.

But then came the news from the scouting parties. Rekshak returned one evening, looking even more angry and sour than usual. "A word, my lord," he said to Hellscream.

"You may speak in front of us all," said Hellscream. They were above ground tonight, enjoying a crisp late autumn evening and feasting upon the kill that Thrall himself had brought back to the clan.

Rekshak cast an uneasy glance in Thrall's direction, then grunted. "As you wish. Humans are beginning to scour the forests. They wear red and gold livery, with a black falcon on their standard."

"Blackmoore," said Thrall, sickened. Would the man never let him be? Was he going to be hunted to the ends of the earth, dragged back in chains to perform again for Blackmoore's twisted amusement?

No. He would take his own life before he would

consent again to a life of slavery. He burned to speak, but courtesy demanded that Hellscream answer his own man.

"As I suspected," said Hellscream, more calmly than Thrall would have thought.

Clearly Rekshak was also taken by surprise. "My lord," he said, "the stranger Thrall has put us all in danger. If they find our caves, then they have us at their mercy. We will either be killed or rounded up like sheep into their camps!"

"Neither shall happen," said Hellscream. "And Thrall has not put us in danger. It was by my decision that he stayed. Do you question that?"

Rekshak lowered his head. "No, my chieftain."

"Thrall shall stay," Hellscream declared.

"With thanks, great chieftain," said Thrall, "Rekshak is right. I must leave. I cannot put the Warsong clan in further danger. I will go and make sure that they have a spurious trail to follow, one that will lead them away from you and yet not lead them to me."

Hellscream leaned closer to Thrall, who was sitting on his right. "But we need you, Thrall," he said. His eyes glowed in the darkness. "*I* need you. We will move quickly, then, to liberate our brothers in the camps."

But Thrall continued to shake his head. "The winter comes. It will be hard to feed an army. And . . . there is something I must do before I am ready to stand at your side to free our brethren. You told me that you knew my clan, the Frostwolves. I must find them and learn more about who I am, where I came from, before I can be ready to stand by your side. I had hoped to travel to them in the spring, but it seems that Blackmoore has forced my hand."

For a long time, Hellscream gazed at Thrall. The bigger orc did not look away from those terrible red eyes. Finally, sadly, Hellscream nodded.

"Though I burn with desire for revenge, I find that yours is the wiser head. Our brothers suffer in confinement, but their lethargy may ease their pain. Time enough when the sun shows its head more brightly to liberate them. I do not know for certain where the Frostwolves dwell, but somehow, I know in my heart that you will find them if you are meant to do so."

"I will depart in the morning," said Thrall, his heart heavy in his chest. Across the flickering fire, he saw Rekshak, who had never liked him, nod in approval.

That next morning Thrall bade a reluctant farewell to the Warsong clan and Grom Hellscream.

"I wish you to have this," said Hellscream, as he lifted a bone necklace from around his too-thin throat. "These are the remains of my first kill. I have carved my symbols in them; any orc chieftain will know them."

Thrall started to object, but Hellscream curled his lips back from his sharp yellow teeth and snarled. Having no desire to displease the chieftain who had been so kind to him, or to hear that ear-splitting scream a second time, Thrall lowered his head so that Grom could place the necklace about his thick neck.

"I will lead the humans away from you," Thrall reiterated.

"If you do not, it is no matter," said Hellscream. "We will tear them limb from limb." He laughed fiercely, and Thrall joined in. Still laughing, he set off in the direction of the cold northlands, the place from which he came.

He made a detour after a few hours, to veer back in the direction of the small village where he had stolen food and frightened the inhabitants. He did not go too near, for his keen ears had already picked up the sound of soldiers' voices. But he did leave a token for Blackmoore's men to find.

Though it nearly killed him to do it, he took the swaddling cloth that bore the mark of the Frostwolves and tore a large strip from it. He placed it carefully to the south of the village on a jagged stump. He wanted it to be easily found, but not too obvious. He also made sure that he left several large, easily traceable footprints in the soft, muddy soil.

With any luck, Blackmoore's men would find the tattered piece of instantly recognizable cloth, see the footprints and assume that Thrall was headed due south. He walked backward carefully in his footprints—a tactic he had learned from his reading—and sought out stone and hard earth for the next several paces.

He looked toward the Alterac Mountains. Grom

had told him that even at the height of summer, their peaks were white against the blue sky. Thrall was about to head into their heart, not knowing for certain where he was going, just as the weather was beginning to turn. It had snowed once or twice, lightly, already. Soon the snows would come thick and heavy, heaviest of all in the mountains.

The Warsong clan had sent him off well supplied. They had given him several strips of dried meat, a waterskin in which he could collect and melt snow, a thick cape to help ward off the worst of the winter's bite, and a few rabbit snares so he could supplement the dried meat.

Fate and luck, and the kindness of strangers and a human girl, had brought him this far. Grom had indicated that Thrall had a role to play yet. He had to trust that, if this was indeed the truth, he would be guided to his destiny as he had been guided thus far.

Hoisting the sack over his back, without a single glance behind him, Thrall began to stride toward the beckoning mountains, whose jagged peaks and hidden valleys were home somewhere to the Frostwolf clan.

TWELVE

The days turned into weeks, and Thrall began to judge how much time had passed not by how many sunrises he saw, but by how many snowfalls. It did not take long for him to exhaust the dried meat the Warsong clan had given him, although he rationed it carefully. The traps proved only intermittently successful, and the farther up in the mountains he went, the fewer animals he caught.

At least water was not a problem. Everywhere around him were icy streams, and then thick, white drifts. More than once he was caught off guard by a sudden storm, and made a burrow in the snow until it passed. Each time, he could only hope that he could dig his way out to safety.

The harsh environment began to take its grim toll. His movements were slower and slower, and more than once he would stop to rest and almost not rise again. The food ran out, and no rabbits or marmots were foolish enough to get caught in his traps. The only way he knew there was any animal life at all was by the occasional print of hoof or paw in the snow, and the eerie howling of distant wolves at night. He began eating leaves and tree bark just to quiet his furious stomach, sometimes with less than digestible results.

Snows came and went, blue skies appeared, dimmed to black, and then clouded over with more snows. He began to despair. He did not even know if he was headed in the right direction to encounter the Frostwolves. He put one foot in front of the other steadily, stubbornly, determined to find his people or die here in these inhospitable mountains.

His mind began to play tricks on him. From time to time, Aedelas Blackmoore would rear out of a snow-drift, screaming harsh words and swinging a broadsword. Thrall could even smell the telltale scent of wine on his breath. They would fight, and Thrall would fall, exhausted, unable to fend off Blackmoore's final blow. It was only then that the shade would disappear, transforming itself from a loathed image into the harmless outline of a rock outcropping or a twisted, weatherworn tree.

Other images were more pleasant. Sometimes Hellscream would come rescue him, offering a warm fire that vanished when Thrall stretched out his hands to it. Other times his rescuer was Sergeant, grumbling about having to track down lost fighters and offering a thick, warm cloak. His sweetest and yet most bitter hallucinations were those when Tari would appear, sympathy in her wide blue eyes and comforting words on her lips. Sometimes she would almost touch him before disappearing before his eyes.

On and on he pressed, until one day, he simply could go no farther. He took one step, and fully intended to take the next, and the one after that, when his body toppled forward of its own accord. His mind tried to command his exhausted, nearly frozen body to rise, but it disobeyed. The snow didn't even feel cold to him anymore. It was . . . warm, and soft. Sighing, Thrall closed his eyes.

A sound made him open them again, but he only stared disinterestedly at this fresh mind-trick. This time it was a large pack of white wolves, almost as white as the snow that surrounded him. They had formed a ring about him, and stood silently, waiting. He stared back, mildly interested in how this scenario would play out. Would they charge, only to vanish? Or would they just wait until unconsciousness claimed him?

Three dark figures loomed up behind the nonexistent wolves. They weren't anyone who had come to visit him before. They were wrapped from head to toe in thick furs. They looked warm, but not as warm as Thrall felt. Their faces were in shadow from fur-trimmed hoods, but he saw large jaws. That and their size marked them as orcs.

He was angry at his mind this time. He had gotten used to the other hallucinations that had visited him. Now he feared he was going to die before finding out what these imaginary people had in store for him.

He closed his eyes, and knew no more.

"I think he's awake." The voice was soft and high-pitched. Thrall stirred and opened heavy-lidded eyes.

Staring right at him with a curious expression on its face was an orc child. Thrall's eyes opened wider to regard the small male. There had been no children among the Warsong clan. They had been cobbled together after dreadful battles, their numbers decimated, and Grom had told him that the children had been the first to succumb.

"Hello," said Thrall in orcish, the word coming out in a harsh rasp. The boy jumped, then laughed.

"He's *definitely* awake," the child said, then scurried away. Another orc loomed into Thrall's field of vision. For the second time in as many minutes, Thrall saw a new type of orc; first the very young one, and now, one who had obviously known many, many winters.

All the features of the orcs were exaggerated in this aged visage. The jowls sagged, the teeth were even yellower than Thrall's, and many were missing or broken. The eyes were a strange milky color, and Thrall could see no pupils in them. This orc's body was twisted and stooped, almost as small as the child's, but Thrall instinctively shrank back from the sheer presence of the elder.

"Hmph," said the old orc. "Thought you were going to die, young one."

Thrall felt a twinge of irritation. "Sorry to disappoint you," he said.

"Our honor code obliges us to help those in need," continued the orc, "but it's always easier if our help proves ineffective. One less mouth to feed."

Thrall was taken aback by the rudeness, but chose to say nothing.

"My name is Drek'Thar. I am the shaman of the Frostwolves, and their protector. Who are you?"

Amusement rippled through Thrall at the idea of this wizened old orc being the protector of all the Frostwolves. He tried to sit up, and was startled to find himself slammed down on the furs as if from an unseen hand. He looked over at Drek'Thar and saw that the old man had subtly changed the position of his fingers.

"I didn't give you leave to rise," said Drek'Thar. "Answer my question, stranger, or I may reconsider our offer of hospitality."

Gazing at the elder with new respect, Thrall said, "My name is Thrall."

Drek'Thar spat. "Thrall! A human word, and a word of subjugation at that."

"Yes," said Thrall, "a word that means slave in their tongue. But I am a thrall no longer, though I keep the name to prick myself to my duties. I have escaped my chains and desire to find out my true history." Without thinking, Thrall tried to sit up again, and was again slammed down. This time, he saw the gnarled old hands twitch slightly. This was a powerful shaman indeed.

"Why did our wolf friends find you wandering in a blizzard?" Drek'Thar demanded. He stared away from Thrall, and Thrall realized that the old orc was blind.

"It is a long story."

"I've got time."

Thrall had to laugh. He found himself liking this cranky old shaman. Surrendering to the implacable force that kept him flat on his back, he told his story. Of how Blackmoore had found him as an infant, had raised him and taught him how to fight and to read. He told the shaman of Tari's kindness, of the listless orcs he had found in the camps, of finally making contact with Hellscream, who had taught him the warrior's code and the language of his people.

"Hellscream was the one who told me that the Frostwolves were my clan," he finished. "He knew by the small piece of cloth in which I was wrapped as a baby. I can show you—" He fell silent, mortified. Of course Drek'Thar could not be "shown" anything.

He expected the shaman to erupt in offense, but instead Drek'Thar extended his hand. "Give it to me."

Now the pressure on his chest eased, and Thrall was able to sit up. He reached in his pack for the tattered remains of the Frostwolf blanket, and wordlessly handed it to the shaman.

Drek'Thar took it in both hands, and brought it to his chest. He murmured softly words Thrall could not catch, and then nodded.

"It is as I suspected," he said, and sighed heavily. He handed the cloth back to Thrall. "The cloth is indeed the pattern of the Frostwolves, and it was woven by the hand of your mother. We had thought you dead."

"How could you tell that—" And then Thrall fully understood what Drek'Thar had said. Hope seized him. "You know my mother? My father? Who am I?"

Drek'Thar lifted his head and stared at Thrall with his blind eyes. "You are the only child of Durotan, our former chieftain, and his courageous mate Draka."

Over a hearty stew of meat, broth, and roots, Drek'Thar told Thrall the rest of his history, at least as much as he knew. He had taken the young orc into his cave, and with the fire burning brightly and thick fur cloaks about their bodies, both old shaman and young warrior were warm and comfortable. Palkar, his attendant, who had been so diligent about alerting him when Thrall had awakened, ladled up the stew and gently pressed the warm wooden bowl into Drek'thar's hands.

The orc ate his stew, delaying speaking. Palkar sat quietly. The only sound was the crackle of the fire and the slow, deep breathing of Wise-ear, Drek'thar's wolf companion. It was a difficult story for Drek'Thar, one he had never imagined he would need to speak of ever again.

"Your parents were the most honored of all the Frostwolves. They left us on a dire errand many winters past, never to return. We did not know what had happened to them . . . until now." He gestured in the direction of the cloth. "The fibers in the cloth have told me. They were slain, and you survived, to be raised by humans."

The cloth was not living, but it had been made of the fur of the white goats that braved the mountains. Because the wool had once belonged to a living being, it had a certain sentience of its own. It could not give details, but it spoke of blood being shed, spattering it with dark red droplets. It also told Drek'Thar a bit about Thrall as well, validating the young orc's story and giving it a sense of truth that Drek'Thar could believe.

He could sense Thrall's doubt that the blanket remnant had "spoken" to him freely. "What was the errand that cost my parents their lives?" the young orc wanted to know.

But that was information Drek'Thar was not ready to share. "I will tell you in time, perhaps. But now, you have put me in a difficult position, Thrall. You come during the winter, the harshest season of all, and as your clan members we must take you in. That does not mean that you will be kept warm, fed, and sheltered without recompense."

"I did not expect to be so treated," said Thrall. "I am

strong. I can work hard, help you hunt. I can teach you some of the ways of humankind, that you will better be prepared to fight them. I can—"

Drek'Thar held up a commanding hand, silencing Thrall's eager babble. He listened. The fire was speaking to him. He leaned in to it, to hear its words better.

Drek'Thar was stunned. Fire was the most undisciplined of the elements. It barely would deign to reply when he addressed it after following all the rituals to appease it. And now, Fire was speaking to him . . . about Thrall!

He saw in his mind images of brave Durotan, beautiful and fierce Draka. *I miss you yet, my old friends,* he thought. *And yet your blood returns to me, in the form of your son. A son of whom even the Spirit of Fire speaks well. But I cannot just give him the mantle of leadership, not as young as he is, as untested . . . as human-tainted!*

"Since your father left, I have been the leader of the Frostwolves," said Drek'Thar. "I accept your offer of aid to the clan, Thrall, son of Durotan. But you will have to earn your rank."

Six days later, as Thrall battled his way through a snowstorm back to the clan encampment with a large, furry animal he and the frost wolves had brought down slung over his back, he wondered if perhaps slavery hadn't been easier.

As soon as the thought struck, he banished it. He was with his own people now, although they continued to regard him with hostility and grudging hospitality. He was always the last to eat. Even the wolves ate their fill before Thrall. He was given the coldest place to sleep, the thinnest cloak, the poorest weapons, the most onerous chores and tasks. He accepted this humbly, recognizing it for what it was: an attempt to test him, to make sure that he had not come to the Frostwolves expecting to be waited on like a king . . . like Blackmoore.

So he covered the refuse pits, skinned the animals, fetched the firewood, and did everything that was asked of him without a word. At least he had the frost wolves to keep him company in the blizzard this time.

One evening, he had asked Drek'Thar about the link between the wolves and the orcs. He was familiar with the concept of domesticating animals, of course, but this seemed different, deeper.

"It is," Drek'Thar replied. "The wolves are not tamed, not as you understand the word. They have come to be our friends because I invited them. It is part of being a shaman. We have a bond with the things of the natural world, and strive always to work in harmony with them. It would be helpful to us if the wolves would be our companions. Hunt with us, keep us warm when the furs are not enough. Alert us to strangers, as they did with you. You would have died had not our wolf friends found you. And in return, we make sure they are well fed, that their injuries are healed, and their cubs need not fear the mighty wind eagles that scour the mountains during the birthing times.

"We have made a similar pact with the goats, although they are not as wise as the wolves. They give us their wool and milk, and when we are in extreme need, one will surrender its life. We protect them in return. They are free to break the pact at any time, but in the last thirty years, none has done so."

Thrall could not believe what he was hearing. This was potent magic indeed. "You link with things other than animals, though, do you not?"

Drek'Thar nodded. "I can call the snows, and wind, and lightning. The trees may bend to me when I ask. The rivers may flow where I ask them to."

"If your power is so great, then why do you continue to live in such a harsh place?" Thrall asked. "If what you are saying is true, you could turn this barren mountaintop into a lush garden. Food would never be difficult to come by, your enemies would never find you—"

"And I would violate the primary agreement with the elements, and nothing of nature would ever respond to me again!" bellowed Drek'Thar. Thrall wished he could snatch back the words, but it was too late. He had obviously deeply offended the shaman. "Do you understand nothing? Have the humans sunk their greedy talons in you so deeply that you cannot see what lies at the heart of a shaman's power? I am granted these things because I *ask*, with respect in my heart, and I am willing to offer something in return. I request only the barest needs for myself and my people. At times, I ask great things, but only when the cause is good and just and wholesome. In return, I thank these powers, knowing that they are borrowed only, never bought. They come to me because they choose to, not because I demand it! These are not slaves, Thrall. They are powerful entities who come of their own free will, who are companions in my magic, not my servants. Pagh!" He snarled and turned away from Thrall. "You will never understand."

For many days, he did not speak with Thrall. Thrall continued to do the lesser jobs, but it seemed that he grew only more distant from the Frostwolves, not closer, as time passed. One evening he was covering the refuse pits when one of the younger males called out, "Slave!"

"My name is Thrall," Thrall said darkly.

The other orc shrugged. "Thrall, slave. It means the same thing. My wolf is ill and has soiled his bedding. Clean it."

Thrall growled low in his throat. "Clean it yourself. I am not your servant, I am a guest of the Frostwolves," he snarled.

"Oh? Really? With a name like slave? Here, human-boy, take it!" He threw a blanket and it covered Thrall before he could react. Cold moisture clung to his face and he smelled the stench of urine.

Something snapped inside him. Red anger flooded his vision and he screamed in outrage. He ripped the filthy blanket off and clenched his fists. He began to stamp, rhythmically, angrily, as he had so long ago in the ring. Only there was no cheering crowd here, only a small circle of suddenly very quiet orcs who stared at him.

The young orc thrust his jaw out stubbornly. "I said, clean it, slave."

Thrall bellowed and sprang. The young male went down, though not without fighting. Thrall didn't feel his flesh part beneath sharp black nails. He felt only the fury, the outrage. He was no one's slave.

Then they were pulling him off and throwing him into a snow bank. The shock of the cold wetness brought him to his senses, and he realized that he had ruined any chance of being accepted by these people. The thought devastated him, and he sat waist-deep in the snow, staring down. He had failed. There was no place that he belonged.

"I had wondered how long it would take you," said Drek'Thar. Thrall glanced up listlessly to see the blind shaman standing over him. "You surprised me by lasting this long."

Slowly, Thrall stood. "I have turned on my hosts," he said heavily. "I will depart."

"You will do no such thing," said Drek'Thar. Thrall turned to stare at him. "The first test I had was to see if you were too arrogant to ask to be one of us. Had you come in here demanding the chieftainship as your birthright, we would have sent you away—and sent our wolves to make sure you stayed away. You needed first to be humble before we would admit you.

"But also, we would not respect anyone who would stay servile for too long. Had you not challenged Uthul's insults, you would not have been a true orc. I am pleased to see you are both humble and proud, Thrall."

Gently, Drek'Thar placed a wizened hand on Thrall's muscular arm. "Both qualities are needed for one who will follow the path of the shaman."

THIRTEEN

Though the rest of that long winter was bitter, Thrall clung to the warmth he felt inside and thought the chill as little. He was accepted now as a member of the clan, and even the Warsongs had not made him feel so valued. Days were spent hunting with clan members who were now family and in listening to Drek'Thar. Nights were spent as part of a loud, happy gathering sitting around a group fire, singing songs and telling tales of past days of glory.

Though Drek'Thar often regaled him with tales of his courageous father Durotan, Thrall somehow sensed that the old orc was holding something back. He did not press the matter, however. Thrall trusted Drek'Thar completely now, and knew that the shaman would tell him what he needed to know, when he needed to know it.

He also made a unique friend. One evening, as the

clan and their wolf companions gathered around the fire as was their usual wont, a young wolf detached itself from the pack that usually slept just beyond the ring of firelight and approached. The Frostwolves fell silent.

"This female will Choose," said Drek'Thar solemnly. Thrall had long since stopped being amazed at how Drek'Thar knew such things as the wolf's gender and its—her—readiness to Choose, whatever that meant. Not without painful effort, Drek'Thar rose and extended his arms toward the she-wolf.

"Lovely one, you wish to form a bond with one of our clan," he said. "Come forward and Choose the one with whom you will be bonded for the rest of your life."

The wolf did not immediately rush forward. She took her time, ears twitching, dark eyes examining every orc present. Most of them already had companions, but many did not, particularly the younger ones. Uthul, who had become Thrall's fast friend once Thrall had rebelled against his cruel treatment, now tensed. Thrall could tell that he wanted this lovely, graceful beast to Choose him.

The wolf's eyes met Thrall's, and it was as if a shock went through his entire body.

The female loped toward Thrall, and lay down at his side. Her eyes bored into his. Thrall felt a warm rush of kinship with this creature, although they were from two different species. He knew, without understanding quite how he knew, that she would be by his side until one of them left this life behind.

Slowly, Thrall reached to touch Snowsong's finely shaped head. Her fur was so soft and thick. A warm wave of pleasure rushed over him.

The group grunted sounds of approval, and Uthul, though keenly disappointed, was the first to clap Thrall on the back.

"Tell us her name," said Drek'Thar.

"Her name is Snowsong," Thrall replied, again, not knowing how he knew. The wolf half-closed her eyes, and he sensed her satisfaction.

Drek'Thar finally revealed the reason for Durotan's death one evening toward the end of winter. More and more, when the sun shone, they heard the sounds of melting snows. Thrall stood by that afternoon and watched respectfully as Drek'Thar performed a ritual to the spring snowmelt, asking that it alter its course only enough to avoid flooding the Frostwolf encampment. As always now, Snowsong stood at his side, a white, silent, faithful shadow.

Thrall felt something stir inside him. He heard a voice: *We hear Drek'Thar's request, and find it not unseemly. We shall not flow where you and yours dwell, Shaman.*

Drek'Thar bowed, and closed the ceremony formally. "I heard it," Thrall said. "I heard the snow answer you."

Drek'Thar turned his unseeing eyes toward Thrall. "I know you heard it," he said. "It is a sign that you are ready, that you have learned and understood all that I have to teach. Tomorrow, you will undergo your initiation. But tonight, come to my cave. I have things to say that you must hear."

When darkness fell, Thrall appeared at the cave. Wise-ear, Drek'Thar's wolf companion, whined happily. Drek'Thar waved Thrall inside.

"Sit," he ordered. Thrall did so. Snowsong went to Wise-ear and they touched noses before curling up and quickly falling asleep. "You have many questions about your father and his fate. I have refrained from answering them, but the time has come that you must know. But first, swear by all you hold dear that you will never tell anyone what I am about to tell you, until you receive a sign that this must be said."

"I swear," said Thrall solemnly. His heart was beating fast. After so many years, he was about to learn the truth.

"You have heard that we were exiled by the late Gul'dan," said Drek'Thar. "What you have not heard is why. No one knew the reason but your parents and myself, and that was as Durotan wished it to be. The fewer people who knew what he knew, the safer his clan."

Thrall said nothing, but hung on Drek'Thar's every word.

"We know now that Gul'dan was evil, and did not have the best interest of the orc people in his heart. What most do not know is how deeply he betrayed us, and what dreadful price we are now paying for what he did to us. Durotan learned, and for that knowledge he was exiled. He and Draka—and you, young Thrall—returned to the southlands to tell the mighty orc chieftain Orgrim Doomhammer of Gul'dan's treachery. We do not know if your parents reached Doomhammer, but we do know that they were murdered for that knowledge."

Thrall bit back the impatient cry, *What knowledge?* Drek'Thar paused for a long moment, then continued.

"Gul'dan only ever wanted power for himself, and he sold us into a sort of slavery to achieve it. He formed a group called the Shadow Council, and this group, comprised of himself and many evil orc warlocks, dictated everything the orcs did. They united with demons, who gave them their vile powers, and who infused the Horde with such a love of killing and fighting that the people forgot the old ways, the way of nature, and the shaman. They lusted only for death. You have seen the red fire in the eyes of the orcs in the camps, Thrall. By that mark, you know that they have been ruled by demon powers."

Thrall gasped. He immediately thought of Hellscream's bright scarlet eyes, of how wasted Hellscream's body was. Yet Hellscream's mind was his own. He had acknowledged the power of mercy, had not given in to either mad bloodlust or the dreadful lethargy he'd seen at the camps. Grom Hellscream must have faced the demons every day, and continued to resist them. Thrall's admiration of the chieftain grew even more as he realized how strong Hellscream's will must be.

"I believe that the lethargy you reported seeing in the camps is the emptiness our people are feeling when the demonic energies have been withdrawn. Without that external energy, they feel weak, bereft. They may not even know why they feel this way, or care enough to ponder it. They are like empty cups, Thrall, that were once filled with poison. Now they cry out to be filled with something wholesome once again. That which they yearn for is the nourishment of the old ways. Shamanism, a reconnection with the simple and pure powers of the natural forces and laws, will fill them again and assuage that dreadful hunger. This, and only this, will rouse them from their stupor and remind them of the proud, courageous line from which we have all come."

Thrall continued to listen raptly, hanging on Drek'Thar's every word.

"Your parents knew of the dark bargain. They knew that this bloodthirsty Horde was as unnatural a construct as could be imagined. The demons and Gul'dan had taken our people's natural courage and warped it, twisted it for their own means. Durotan knew this, and for that knowledge his clan was banished. He accepted that, but when you were born, he knew he could no longer remain silent. He wanted a better world for you, Thrall. You were his son and heir. You would have been the next chieftain. He and Draka went into the southlands, as I have told you, to find their old friend Orgrim Doomhammer."

"I know that name," said Thrall. "He was the mighty Warchief who led all the clans together against the humans."

Drek'Thar nodded. "He was wise and brave, a good leader of our people. The humans eventually were the victors, Gul'dan's treachery—at least a pale shadow of its true depths—was discovered, and the demons withdrew. You know the rest."

"Was Doomhammer killed?"

"We do not believe so, but nothing has been heard from him since. The odd rumor reaches us now and then, that he has become a hermit, gone into hiding, or that he has been taken prisoner. Many think of him as a legend, who will return to free us when the time is right."

Thrall looked carefully at his teacher. "And what is it you think, Drek'Thar?"

The old orc chuckled deep in his throat. "I think," he said, "that I have told you enough, and that it is time for you to rest. The morrow will bring your initiation, if it is meant to be. You'd best be prepared."

Thrall rose and bowed respectfully. Even if the shaman could not see the gesture, he made it, for himself. "Come, Snowsong," he called, and the white wolf padded obediently into the night with her life's companion.

* * *

Drek'Thar listened, and when he was certain they had gone, he called to Wise-ear. "I have a task for you, my friend. You know what to do."

Although he had tried to get as much rest as he could, Thrall found sleep elusive. He was too excited, too apprehensive, about what his initiation would bring. Drek'Thar had told him nothing. He wished desperately he had some kind of idea as to what to expect.

He was wide awake when the gray dawn filled his cave with faint light. He rose and made his way outside, and was surprised to find that everyone else was awake and gathered silently outside his cave.

Thrall opened his mouth to speak, but Drek'Thar held up a commanding hand. "You are not to speak again until I give you leave," he said. "Depart at once, to go alone into the mountains. Snowsong must stay. You are not to eat or drink, but think hard about the path upon which you are about to set foot. When the sun has set, return to me, and the rite will begin."

Obediently, Thrall turned at once and left. Snowsong, knowing what was expected of her, did not follow. She did throw her head back and begin to howl. All the other wolves joined in, and the savage, sweet chorus accompanied Thrall as he went, alone, to meditate.

The day passed more swiftly than he would have expected. His mind was filled with questions, and he was surprised when the light changed and the sun, orange against the winter sky, began to move toward the horizon. He returned just as its last rays bathed the encampment.

Drek'Thar was waiting for him. Thrall noticed that Wise-ear was nowhere to be seen, which was unusual, but he assumed that this was part of the rite. Snowsong was also not present. He approached Drek'Thar and waited. The old orc gestured that Thrall follow.

He led Thrall over a snow-covered ridge to an area that Thrall had never seen before. In answer to the unvoiced question, Drek'Thar replied, "This place has always been here, but it does not wish to be seen. Therefore, only now, when it welcomes you, is it visible to you."

Thrall felt nervousness rise in him, but refrained from speaking. Drek'Thar waved his hands, and the snow melted right before Thrall's eyes, leaving a large, circular, rocky platform. "Stand in the center, Thrall, son of Durotan," said Drek'Thar. His voice was no longer raspy and quavering, but was filled with a power and authority Thrall had never heard from him before. He obeyed.

"Prepare to meet the spirits of the natural world," said Drek'Thar, and Thrall's heart leaped.

Nothing happened. He waited. Still nothing happened. He shifted, uneasily. The sun had fully set and the stars were beginning to appear. He was growing impatient and angry when a voice spoke very loudly inside his head: *Patience is the first test.*

Thrall inhaled swiftly. The voice spoke again.

I am the Spirit of Earth, Thrall, son of Durotan. I am the soil that yields the fruit, the grasses that feed the beasts. I am the rock, the bones of this world. I am all that grows and lives in my womb, be it worm or tree or flower. Ask me.

Ask you what? thought Thrall.

There was a strange sensation, almost as of a warm chuckle. *Knowing the question is part of your test.*

Thrall panicked, then calmed himself, as Drek'Thar had taught. A question came calmly into his mind:

Will you lend me your strength and power when I need it, for the good of the Clan and those we would aid?

Ask, came the reply.

Thrall began to stamp his feet. He felt power rising inside him, as he always did, but for the first time it was not accompanied by bloodlust. It was warm and strong and he felt as solid as the bones of the earth themselves. He was barely aware of the very earth trembling beneath him, and it was only when an unbearably sweet scent filled his nostrils that he opened his eyes.

The earth had erupted into enormous fissures, and on every inch of what was rock, flowers bloomed. Thrall gaped.

I have agreed to lend you my assistance, for the good of the Clan and those you would aid. Honor me, and that gift shall always be yours.

Thrall felt the power recede, leaving him trembling with shock at what he had summoned and controlled. But he had only a moment to marvel at it, for another voice was in his head now.

I am the Spirit of Air, Thrall, son of Durotan. I am the winds that warm and cool the earth, that which fills your lungs and keeps you alive. I carry the birds and insects and dragons, and all things that dare soar to my challenging heights. Ask me.

Thrall knew what to do this time, and asked the same question. The sensation of power that filled him was different this time: lighter, freer. Even though he had been forbidden to speak, he could not help the laughter that bubbled forth from his soul. He felt warm winds caress him, bringing all manner of delicious scents to his nostrils, and when he opened his eyes, he was floating high above the ground. Drek'Thar was so far below him he seemed as a child's toy. But Thrall was not afraid. The Spirit of Air would support him; he had asked, and it had answered.

Gently, he floated down, until he felt the solid stone beneath his feet. Air caressed him with a gentle touch, then dissipated.

Power again filled Thrall, and this time it was almost painful. Heat churned in his belly, and sweat popped out on his green skin. He felt an almost overpowering desire to leap into the nearby snowbanks. The Spirit of Fire was here, and he asked for its aid. It responded.

There was a loud crackling overhead, and Thrall, startled by the sound, looked up. Lightning danced its dangerous dance across the night sky. Thrall knew that it was his to command. The flowers that had strewn the broken earth exploded into flames, crisp-ing and burning to ashes in the space of a few heart-beats. This was a dangerous element, and Thrall thought of the pleasant fires that had kept his clan alive. At once, the fires went out, to re-form in a small, contained, cozy area.

Thrall thanked the Spirit of Fire, and felt its presence depart. He was feeling drained by all this strange energy alternately coursing through him and then departing, and was grateful that there was only one more element to acknowledge.

The Spirit of Water flowed into him, calming and cooling the burn the Spirit of Fire had left behind. Thrall had a vision of the ocean, though he had never seen one before, and extended his mind to probe its darkling depths. Something cold touched his skin. He opened his eyes to see that it was snowing thick and fast. With a thought, he turned it to rain, and then halted it altogether. The comfort of the Spirit of Water within him soothed and strengthened, and he let it go with deep, heartfelt thanks.

He looked over at Drek'Thar, but the shaman shook his head. "Your test is not yet completed," he said.

And then suddenly Thrall was shaken from head to toe with such a rush of power that he gasped aloud. Of course. The fifth element.

The Spirit of the Wilds.

We are the Spirit of the Wilds, the essence and souls of all things living. We are the most powerful of all, surpassing the quakes of Earth, the winds of Air, the flames of Fire, and the

floods of Water. Speak, Thrall, and tell us why you think you
are worthy of our aid.

Thrall couldn't breathe. He was overwhelmed by
the power churning within and without him. Forcing
his eyes to open, he saw pale white shapes swirling
about him. One was a wolf, the other a goat, another
an orc, and a human, and a deer. He realized that
every living thing had spirits, and felt despair rise up in
him at the thought of having to sense and control all of
them.

But faster than he could have dreamed, the spirits
filled and then vacated him. Thrall felt pummeled by
the onslaught, but forced himself to try to focus, to address each one with respect. It became impossible and
he sank to his knees.

A soft sound filled the air, and Thrall struggled to lift
a head that felt as heavy as stone.

They floated calmly around him now, and he knew
that he had been judged and found worthy. A ghostly
stag pranced about him, and he knew that he would
never simply be able to bite into a haunch of venison
without feeling its Spirit, and thanking it for the nourishment it provided. He felt a kinship with every orc
that had ever been born, and even the human Spirit felt
more like Taretha's sweet presence than Blackmoore's
dark cruelty. Everything was bright, even if sometimes
it embraced the dark; all life was connected, and any
shaman who tampered with the chain without the utmost care and respect for that Spirit was doomed to fail.

Then they were gone. Thrall fell forward, utterly drained. He felt Drek'Thar's hand on his shoulder, shaking him. The old shaman assisted Thrall in sitting up. Thrall had never felt so limp and weak in his life.

"Well done, my child," said Drek'Thar, his voice trembling with emotion. "I had hoped they would accept . . . Thrall, you must know. It has been years, nay, decades, since the spirits have accepted a shaman. They were angry with us for our warlocks' dark bargain, their corruption of magic. There are only a few shamans left now, and all are as old as I. The spirits have waited for someone worthy upon whom to bestow their gifts; you are the first in a long, long time to be so honored. I had feared that the spirits would forever refuse to work with us again, but . . . Thrall, I have never seen a stronger shaman in my life, and you are only beginning."

"I . . . I thought it would feel so powerful," stammered Thrall, his voice faint. "But instead . . . I am so humbled. . . ."

"And it is that which makes you worthy." He reached and stroked Thrall's cheek. "Durotan and Draka would be so proud of you."

FOURTEEN

With the Spirits of Earth, Air, Fire, Water and the Wilds as his willing companions, Thrall felt stronger and more confident than ever in his life. He worked together with Drek'Thar to learn the specific "calls," as the elder called them. "Warlocks would term them spells," he told Thrall, "but we—shamans—term them simply 'calls.' We ask, the powers we work with answer. Or not, as they will."

"Have they ever not answered?" asked Thrall.

Drek'Thar was silent. "Yes," he answered slowly. They were sitting together in Drek'Thar's cave, talking late at night. These conversations were precious to Thrall, and always enlightening.

"When? Why?" Thrall wanted to know, then immediately added, "Unless you do not wish to speak of it."

"You are a shaman now, although a fledgling one,"

said Drek'Thar. "It is right that you understand our limitations. I am ashamed to admit that I asked for improper things more than once. The first time, I asked for a flood to destroy an encampment of humans. I was angry and bitter, for they had destroyed many of our clan. But there were many wounded and even women and children at this place, and Water would not do it."

"But floods happen all the time," said Thrall. "Many innocents die, and it serves no purpose."

"It serves the Spirit of Water's purpose, and the Wilds'," replied Drek'Thar. "I do not know their needs and plans. They certainly do not tell me of them. This time, it did not serve Water's needs, and it would not flood and drown hundreds of humans it saw as innocent. Later, once the rage had faded, I understood that the Spirit of Water was right."

"When else?"

Drek'Thar hesitated. "You probably assume I have always been old, guiding the clan spiritually."

Thrall chuckled. "No one is born old, Wise One."

"Sometimes I wish I had been. But I was once young, as you are, and the blood flowed hot in my veins. I had a mate and child. They died."

"In battle against the humans?"

"Nothing so noble. They simply fell ill, and all my pleas to the elements were to no avail. I raged in my grief." Even now, his voice was laden with sorrow. "I demanded that the spirits return the lives they had snatched. They grew angry with me, and for many years, refused my call. Because of my arrogant demand that my loved ones come back to life, many others of our clan suffered from my inability to summon the spirits. When I saw the foolishness of my request, I begged the spirits to forgive me. They did."

"But . . . it is only natural to want your loved ones to stay alive," said Thrall. "Surely the spirits must understand that."

"Oh, they understood. My first request was humble, and the element listened with compassion before it refused. My next request was a furious demand, and the Spirit of the Wilds was offended that I so abused the relationship between shaman and element."

Drek'Thar extended a hand and placed it on Thrall's shoulder. "It is more than likely you will endure the pain of losing loved ones, Thrall. You must know that the Spirit of the Wilds has reasons for doing what it does, and you must respect those reasons."

Thrall nodded, but privately he completely sympathized with Drek'Thar's desires, and did not blame the old orc one bit for raging at the spirits in his torment.

"Where is Wise-ear?" he asked, to change the subject.

"I don't know." Drek'Thar seemed singularly unconcerned. "He is a companion, not a slave. He leaves when he wishes, returns when it is his will."

As if to reassure him that she was not about to go anywhere, Snowsong placed her head on Thrall's knee.

He patted her head, bade his teacher good night, and went to his own cave to sleep.

The days passed in a routine fashion. Thrall now spent most of his time studying with Drek'Thar, though on occasion he went hunting with a small group. He utilized his newfound relationship with the elements to aid his clan: asking the Spirit of Earth for advice on where the herds were, asking the Spirit of Air to change the course of the wind so that their scent would not betray them to the watchful creatures. Only once did he ask the Spirit of the Wilds for aid, when supplies were running dangerously low and their luck in hunting had taken a turn for the worse.

They knew deer were in the area. They had found gnawed tree bark and fresh droppings. But the canny creatures continued to elude them for several days. Their bellies were empty, and there was simply no more food left. The children were beginning to grow dangerously thin.

Thrall closed his eyes and extended his mind. *Spirit of the Wilds, who breathes life into all, I ask for your favor. We will take no more than we need to feed the hungry of our clan. I ask you, Spirit of the deer, to sacrifice yourself for us. We will not waste any of your gifts, and we will honor you. Many lives depend upon the surrendering of one.*

He hoped the words were right. They had been couched with a respectful heart, but Thrall had never attempted this before. But when he opened his eyes, he saw a white stag standing not two arms' length in front of him. His companions seemed to see nothing. The stag's eyes met Thrall's, and the creature inclined its head. It bounded away, and Thrall saw that it left no trace in the snow.

"Follow me," he said. His fellow Frostwolves did so at once, and they went some distance before they saw a large, healthy stag lying in the snow. One of its legs jutted out at an unnatural angle, and its soft brown eyes were rolling in terror. The snow all around it was churned up, and it was obvious that it was unable to rise.

Thrall approached it, instinctively sending out a message of calm. *Do not fear,* he told it. *Your pain will soon be ended, and your life continue to have meaning. I thank you, Brother, for your sacrifice.*

The deer relaxed, and lowered its head. Thrall touched its neck gently. Quickly, to cause it no pain, he snapped the long neck. He looked up to see the others staring at him in awe. But he knew it was not by his will, but the deer's, that his people would eat tonight.

"We will take this animal and consume its flesh. We will make tools from the bones and clothing from its hide. And in so doing, we will remember that it honored us with this gift."

Thrall worked side by side with Drek'Thar to send energy to the seeds beneath the soil, that they would grow strong and flower in the spring that was so near, and to nurture the unborn beasts, be they deer or goat or wolf, growing in their mothers' wombs. They worked together to ask Water to spare the village from the spring snowmelts and the avalanches that were a constant danger. Thrall grew steadily in strength and in skill, and was so engrossed in this new, vibrant path he was walking that when he saw the first yellow and purple spring flowers poking their heads up through the melting snows, he was taken by surprise.

When he returned from his walk to gather the sacred herbs that aided the shaman's contact with the elements, he was surprised to find that the Frostwolves had another guest.

This orc was large, though from weight or muscle, Thrall could not say as the stranger's cloak was wrapped tightly around him. He huddled close to the fire and seemed not to feel the spring warmth.

Snowsong rushed forward to sniff noses and tails with Wise-ear, who had at long last returned. Thrall turned to Drek'Thar.

"Who is the stranger?" he asked softly.

"A wandering hermit," Drek'Thar replied. "We do not know him. He says that Wise-ear found him lost in the mountains, and led him here to safety."

Thrall looked at the bowl of stew the stranger clutched in one big hand, at the polite concern shown to him by the rest of the clan. "You receive him with more kindness than you received me," he said, not a little annoyed.

Drek'Thar laughed. "He comes asking only for

refuge for a few days before pressing on. He didn't come with a torn Frostwolf swaddling cloth asking to be adopted by the clan. And he comes at springtime, when there is bounty to be had and shared, and not at the onset of winter."

Thrall had to acknowledge the shaman's points. Anxious to behave properly, he sat down by the stranger. "Greetings, stranger. How long have you been traveling?"

The orc looked at him from under a shadowing hood. His gray eyes were sharp, though his answer was polite, even deferential.

"Longer than I care to recall, young one. I am in your debt. I had thought the Frostwolves only a legend, told by Gul'dan's cronies to intimidate all other orcs."

Clan loyalty stirred inside Thrall. "We were banished wrongly, and have proved our worth by being able to make a life for ourselves in this harsh place," he replied.

"But it is my understanding that not so long ago, you were as much a stranger to this clan as I," the stranger said. "They have spoken of you, young Thrall."

"I hope they have spoken well," Thrall answered, unsure as to how to respond.

"Well enough," the stranger replied, enigmatically. He returned to eating his stew. Thrall saw that his hands were well muscled.

"What is your own clan, friend?"

The hand froze with the spoon halfway to the mouth. "I have no clan, now. I wander alone."

"Were they all killed?"

"Killed, or taken, or dead where it counts . . . in the soul," the orc answered, pain in his voice. "Let us speak no more of this."

Thrall inclined his head. He was uncomfortable around the stranger, and suspicious as well. Something was not quite right about him. He rose, nodded his head, and went to Drek'Thar.

"We should watch him," he said to his teacher. "There is something about this wandering hermit that I mislike."

Drek'Thar threw back his head and laughed. "We were wrong to suspect you when you came, yet you are the only one who mistrusts this hungry stranger. Oh, Thrall, you have yet so much to learn."

Over dinner that night, Thrall continued to watch the stranger without appearing too obvious. He had a large sack, which he would let no one touch, and never removed the bulky cape. He answered questions politely, but briefly, and revealed very little about himself. All Thrall knew was that he had been a hermit for twenty years, keeping to himself and nursing dreams of the old days without appearing to do very much to actually help bring them back.

At one point, Uthul asked, "Have you ever seen the internment camps? Thrall says the orcs imprisoned there have lost their will."

"Yes, and it is no surprise that this is so," said the stranger. "There is little to fight for anymore."

"There is much to fight for," said Thrall, his anger

flaring quickly. "Freedom. A place of our own. The remembrance of our origins."

"And yet you Frostwolves hide up here in the mountains," the stranger replied.

"As you hide in the southlands!" Thrall retorted.

"I do not purport to rouse the orcs to cast off their slaves and revolt against their masters," the stranger replied, his voice calm, not rising to the bait.

"I will not be here long," said Thrall. "Come spring, I will rejoin the undefeated orc chieftain Grom Hellscream, and help his noble Warsong clan storm the camps. We will inspire our brethren to rise up against the humans, who are not their masters, but merely bullies who keep them against their will!" Thrall was on his feet now, the anger hot inside him at the insult this stranger dared to utter. He kept expecting Drek'Thar to chide him, but the old orc said nothing. He merely stroked his wolf companion and listened. The other Frostwolves seemed fascinated by the interchange between these two and did not interrupt.

"Grom Hellscream," sneered the stranger, waving his hand dismissively. "A demon-ridden dreamer. No, you Frostwolves have the right of it, as do I. I have seen what the humans can do, and it is best to avoid them, and seek the hidden places where they do not come."

"I was raised by humans, and believe me, they are not infallible!" cried Thrall. "Nor are you, I would think, you coward!"

"Thrall—" began Drek'Thar, speaking up at last.

"No, Master Drek'Thar, I will not be silent. This . . . this . . . he comes seeking our aid, eats at our fire, and dares to insult the courage of our clan and his own race. I will not stand for it. I am not the chieftain, nor do I claim that right, though I was born to it. But I will claim my individual right to fight this stranger, and make him eat his words sliced upon my sword!"

He expected the cowardly hermit to cringe and ask his pardon. Instead, the stranger laughed heartily and rose. He was almost as big as Thrall, and now, finally, Thrall could glimpse beneath the cloak. To his astonishment, he saw that this arrogant stranger was completely clad in black plate armor, trimmed with brass. Once, the armor must have been stunning, but though it was still impressive, the plates had seen better days and the brass trim was sorely in need of polishing.

Uttering a fierce cry, the stranger opened the pack he had been carrying and pulled out the largest warhammer Thrall had ever seen. He held it aloft with seeming ease, then brandished it at Thrall.

"See if you can take me, whelp!" he cried.

The other orcs cried aloud as well, and for the second time in as many moments Thrall received a profound shock. Instead of leaping to the defense of their clansman, the Frostwolves backed away. Some even fell to their knees. Only Snowsong stayed with him, putting herself between her companion and the stranger, hackles raised and white teeth bared.

What was happening? He glanced over at Drek'Thar, who seemed relaxed and impassive.

So be it, then. Whoever this stranger might be, he had insulted Thrall and the Frostwolves, and the young shaman was prepared to defend his honor and theirs with his life.

He had no weapon ready, but Uthul pressed a long, sharp spear into Thrall's outstretched hand. Thrall's fingers closed on it, and he began to stamp.

Thrall could feel the Spirit of the Earth responding questioningly. As gently as he could, for he had no wish to upset the element, he declined an offer of aid. This was not a battle for the elements; there was no dire need here. Only Thrall's need to teach this arrogant stranger a sorely needed lesson.

Even so, he felt the earth tremble beneath his pounding feet. The stranger looked startled, then oddly pleased. Before Thrall could even brace himself, the armored stranger launched into a punishing attack.

Thrall's spear came up to defend himself, but while it was a fierce weapon, it was never meant to block the blow of an enormous warhammer. The mighty spear snapped in two as if it were a twig. Thrall glanced around, but there was no other weapon. He prepared for his adversary's next blow, deciding to utilize the strategy that had worked so well for him in the past when he was fighting weaponless against an armed opponent.

The stranger swung his hammer again. Thrall

dodged it, and whirled deftly to reach out and seize the weapon, planning to snatch it from its wielder. To his astonishment, as his hands closed on the shaft, the stranger tugged swiftly. Thrall fell forward, and the stranger straddled his now fallen body.

Thrall twisted like a fish, and managed to hurl himself to the side while catching one of his foe's legs tightly between his ankles. He jerked, and the stranger staggered and lost his balance. Now they were both on the earth. Thrall slammed his clenched fist down on the wrist of the hand that clutched the warhammer. The stranger grunted and reflexively loosed his hold. Seizing the opportunity and the warhammer both, Thrall leaped to his feet, swinging the weapon high over his head.

He caught himself just in time. He was about to bring the massive stone weapon crunching down on his opponent's skull. But this was a fellow orc, not a human he faced on the battlefield. This was a guest in his encampment, and a warrior he would be proud to have serve alongside him when he and Hellscream achieved their goal of storming the encampments and liberating their imprisoned kin.

The hesitation and the sheer weight of the weapon caused him to stumble. That moment was all the stranger needed. Growling, he utilized the same move Thrall had used on him. He kicked forward, knocking Thrall's feet out from under him. Still clutching the warhammer, Thrall fell, unable to stop himself. Before he even realized what was happening, the other orc was on top of him with his hands at Thrall's throat.

Thrall's world went red. Instinct kicked in and he writhed. This orc was almost as large as he and armored as well, but Thrall's fierce desire for victory and extra bulk gave him the edge he needed to twist his body around and pin the other warrior beneath him.

Hands closed on him and pulled him off. He roared, the hot bloodlust in him demanding satisfaction, and struggled. It took eight of his fellow Frostwolves to pin him down long enough for the red haze to clear and his breathing to slow. When he nodded that he was all right, they rose and let him sit up on his own.

Before him stood the stranger. He stomped forward and shoved his face to within a hand's breadth of Thrall's. Thrall met his eyes evenly, panting with exertion.

The stranger drew himself up to his full height and then let out a huge roar of laughter.

"Long has it been since anyone could even *challenge* me," he bellowed cheerfully, not seeming the least displeased that Thrall had nearly managed to smear his entrails into the earth. "And it has been even longer since anyone could best me, even in a friendly tussle. Only your father ever did that, young Thrall. May his spirit walk in peace. Hellscream did not lie, it seems I appear to have found my second in command."

He extended a hand to Thrall. Thrall stared at it, and snapped, "Second in command? I beat you, stranger, with your own weapon. I know not what code makes the victor second!"

"Thrall!" Drek'Thar's voice cracked like a lightning strike.

"He does not yet understand," chuckled the stranger. "Thrall, son of Durotan, I have come a long way to find you, to see if the rumors were true—that there was yet a worthy second in command for me to take under my wing and trust in when I liberate the encampments."

He paused, and his eyes twinkled with laughter.

"My name, son of Durotan, is Orgrim Doomhammer."

FIFTEEN

Thrall's mouth dropped open in chagrin and shock. He had insulted Orgrim Doomhammer, the Warchief of the Horde? His father's dearest friend? The one orc he had held up as inspiration for so many years? The armor and the warhammer ought to have given the game away at once. What a fool he had been!

He fell to his knees and prostrated himself. "Most noble Doomhammer, I ask your forgiveness. I did not know—" He shot a look at Drek'Thar. "My teacher might have warned me—"

"And that would have spoiled everything," Doomhammer replied, still laughing a little. "I wanted to pick a fight, see if you indeed had the passion and the pride of which Grom Hellscream had spoken so glowingly. I got more than I bargained for . . . I got beaten!" He laughed again, loudly, as if were the funniest thing that had happened to him in years. Thrall began to relax. Doomhammer's mirth subsided and he placed an affectionate hand on the younger orc's shoulder.

"Come and sit with me, Thrall, son of Durotan," he said. "We will finish our meal and you will tell me your story, and I will tell you tales of your father you have never heard."

Joy flooded Thrall. Impulsively he reached out and gripped the hand that lay on his shoulder. Suddenly serious, Doomhammer met Thrall's eyes and nodded.

Now that everyone knew who the mysterious stranger truly was—Drek'Thar confessed that he had known all along, and indeed had sent Wise-ear to find Doomhammer for just this confrontational purpose— the Frostwolves were able to treat their honored guest with the respect due him. They brought out several hares they had planned on drying for later use, dressed them with precious oils and herbs, and began to roast them over the fire. More herbs were added to the flame, and their pungent, sweet scents rose with the smoke. It was almost intoxicating. Drums and pipes were brought out, and soon the sounds of music and singing rose up to entwine with the smoke, sending a message of honoring and joy to the spirit worlds.

Thrall was tongue-tied at first, but Doomhammer coaxed his story out of him by alternately listening closely and asking probing questions. When Thrall was done, he did not speak at once.

"This Blackmoore," he said. "He sounds like Gul'dan. One who does not have the best interests of his people in his heart, but only his own profit and pleasure."

Thrall nodded. "I was not the only one to experience his cruelty and unpredictability. I am certain that he hates orcs, but he has little love for his own people either."

"And this Taretha, and Sergeant . . . I did not know humans were capable of such things as kindness and honor."

"I would not have known of honor and mercy had it not been for Sergeant," said Thrall. Amusement rippled through him. "Nor would I have known that first maneuver I used on you. It has won me the battle many times."

Doomhammer chuckled with him, then sobered. "It has been my experience that the males hate our people, and the females and children fear us. Yet this girl-child, of her own will, befriended you."

"She has a great heart," Thrall said. "I can give her no higher compliment than to say that I would be proud to admit her into my clan. She has an orc's spirit, tempered by compassion."

Doomhammer was silent again for a time. Finally, he said, "I have kept to myself these many years, since the final, ignominious defeat. I know what they say about me. I am a hermit, a coward, afraid to show my face. Do you know why I have scorned the company of others until this night, Thrall?"

Thrall silently shook his head.

"Because I needed to be by myself, to analyze what had happened. To think. To remind myself who I was, who we were as a people. From time to time, I would do as I have done this night. I would venture forth to the campfires, accept their hospitality, listen to their experiences, and learn." He paused. "I know the insides of human prisons, as you do. I was captured and kept as an oddity by King Terenas of Lordaeron for a time. I escaped from his palace, as you escaped from Durnholde. I was even in an encampment. I know what it is like to be that broken, that despairing. I almost became one of them."

He had been staring into the fire as he spoke. Now he turned to look at Thrall. Though his gray eyes were clear and devoid of the evil flame that burned in Hellscream's eyes, by a trick of the firelight, his eyes now seemed to gleam as red as Grom's.

"But I did not. I escaped, just as you did. I found it easy, just as you did. And yet it remains difficult for those huddled in the mud in those encampments. We can only do so much from the outside. If a pig loves her stall, the open door means nothing. So it is with those in the camps. They must want to walk through the door when we open it for them."

Thrall was beginning to see what Doomhammer was trying to say. "Tearing down the walls alone will not ensure our people's freedom," he said.

Doomhammer nodded. "We must remind them of the way of the shaman. They must rid their contaminated spirits of the poison of the demon-whispered words, and instead embrace their true natures of the warrior and the spirit. You have won the admiration of the Warsong clan, and their fierce leader, Thrall. Now you have the Frostwolves, the most independent and proud clan I have ever known, ready to follow you into battle. If there is any orc living that can teach our broken kindred to remember who they are, it is you."

Thrall thought of the encampment, of its dreary, deadly sloth. He also thought of how narrowly he had escaped Blackmoore's men.

"Though I despise the place, I will willingly return, if I can hope to reawaken my people," Thrall said. "But you must know that my capture is something that Blackmoore deeply desires. Twice, I have only narrowly escaped him. I had hoped to lead a charge against him, but—"

"But that will fail, without troops," Doomhammer said. "I know these things, Thrall. Though I have been a lone wanderer, I have not been inattentive to what has been happening in the land. Do not worry. We will lay false trails for Blackmoore and his men to follow."

"The commanders of the camps know to look for me," said Thrall.

"They will be looking for large, powerful, spirited, intelligent Thrall," countered Doomhammer. "Another defeated, muddied, broken orc will be overlooked. Can you hide that stubborn pride, my friend? Can you bury it and pretend that you have no spirit, no will of your own?"

"It will be difficult," Thrall admitted, "but I will do it, if it will help my people."

"Spoken like the true son of Durotan," said Doomhammer, his voice oddly thick.

Thrall hesitated, but pressed on. He had to know as much as he could. "Drek'Thar tells me that Durotan and Draka left to seek you, to convince you that Gul'dan was evil and using the orcs only to further his own struggle for power. The cloth in which I was wrapped told Drek'Thar that they had died violently, and I know that I was alone with the bodies of two orcs and a white wolf when Blackmoore found me. Please . . . can you tell me . . . did my father find you?"

"He did," Doomhammer said heavily. "And it is my greatest shame and sorrow that I did not keep them closer. I thought it for the good of both my warriors and Durotan as well. They came, bringing you, young Thrall, and told me of Gul'dan's treachery. I believed them. I knew of a place where they would be safe, or so I thought. I later learned that several of my own warriors were Gul'dan's spies. Though I do not know for certain, I am convinced that the guard I entrusted to lead Durotan to safety summoned assassins to kill them instead." Doomhammer sighed deeply, and for a moment it seemed to Thrall as if the weight of the world was piled atop those broad, powerful shoulders.

"Durotan was my friend. I would gladly have given

my life for him and his family. Yet I unwittingly caused their deaths. I can only hope to atone for that by doing everything I can for the child he left behind. You come from a proud and noble line, Thrall, despite the name which you have chosen to keep. Let us honor that line together."

A few weeks later, in the full bloom of spring, Thrall found it ease itself to lumber into a village, roar at the farmers, and let himself be captured. Once the trap-net had closed about him, he subsided, whimpering, to make his captors believe that they had crushed his spirit.

Even when he was set free in the encampment, he was careful not to give himself away. But once the guards had ceased regarding him as a novelty, Thrall began to speak softly to those who would listen. He had singled out the few who still seemed to have spirit. In the darkness, with the human guards nodding at their posts, Thrall told these orcs of their origins. He spoke of the powers of the shamans, of his own skills. More than once, a skeptic demanded proof. Thrall did not make the earth shake, or call the thunder and lightning. Instead, he picked up a handful of mud, and sought what was left of life within it. Before the astonished eyes of the captives, he caused the brown earth to sprout forth grasses and even flowers.

"Even what appears dead and ugly has power and beauty," Thrall told the awestruck watchers. They turned to him, and his heart leaped within him as h saw the faintest glimmerings of hope in their expressions.

While Thrall subjected himself to voluntary imprisonment in order to inspire the beaten, imprisoned orcs in the camps, the Frostwolf clan and the Warsong clan had joined forces under Doomhammer. They watched the camp which Thrall was in, and waited for his signal.

It took longer than Thrall had hoped to rouse the downtrodden orcs to even think of rebellion, but eventually, he decided the time was right. In the small hours of the morning, when the light snoring of many of the guards could be heard in the dewy hush, Thrall knelt on the good, solid soil. He lifted his hands and asked the Spirits of Water and Fire to come to help him free his people.

They came.

A soft rain began falling. Suddenly the sky was split with three jagged lines of lightning. A pause, then the display was repeated. Angry thunder rolled after each one, almost shaking the earth. This was the agreed-upon signal. The orcs waited, frightened yet excited, clutching the makeshift weapons of stones and sticks and other things that could be readily found in the encampment. They waited for Thrall to tell them what to do.

A terrifying scream split the night more piercingly than the thunder, and Thrall's heart soared. He would recognize that cry anywhere—it was Grom Hellscream. The sound startled the orcs, but Thrall cried over the din, "Those are our allies outside the walls! They have come to free us!"

The guards had been awakened by the thunderclaps. Now they scrambled to their posts as Hellscream's cries faded, but they were too late. Thrall asked again for lightning, and it came.

A jagged bolt of it struck the main wall, where most of the guards were posted. Mixed in with that terrible sound were a clap of thunder and the screams of the guards. Thrall blinked in the sudden darkness, but there were tongues of flame still burning here and there, and he could see that the wall was completely breached.

Over that breach spilled a tide of lithe green bodies. They charged the guards and overwhelmed them with almost casual ease. The orcs gaped at the sight.

"Can you feel it stirring?" Thrall yelled. "Can you feel your spirits longing to fight, to kill, to be free? Come, my brothers and sisters!" Without looking to see if they followed, Thrall charged toward the opening.

He heard their tentative voices behind him, growing in volume with each step they took toward liberation. Suddenly Thrall grunted in pain as something impaled his arm. A black-fletched arrow had sunk almost the entire way through it. He ignored the pain; time enough to tend to it when all were free.

There was fighting all around him, the sounds of steel striking sword and ax biting flesh. Some of the guards, the more intelligent ones, had realized what was happening and were rushing to block the exit with their own bodies. Thrall spared a moment of pity for the futility of their deaths, then charged.

He snatched up a weapon from a fallen comrade and beat back the inexperienced guard easily. "Go, go!" he cried, waving with his left hand. The imprisoned orcs first froze in a tight group, then one of them yelled and charged forward. The rest followed. Thrall lifted his weapon, brought it down, and the guard fell writhing into the bloody mud.

Gasping from exertion, Thrall looked around. All he could see now were the Warsong and Frostwolf clans engaged in combat. There were no more prisoners.

"Retreat!" he cried, and made for the pile of still-hot rocks that had once been imprisoning walls and the sweet darkness of the night. His clansmen followed. There were one or two guards who gave chase, but the orcs were faster and soon outdistanced them.

The agreed-upon meeting place was an ancient pile of standing stones. The night was dark, but orcish eyes did not need the moons' illumination to see. By the time Thrall reached the site, dozens of orcs were huddled by the eight towering stones.

"Success!" cried a voice at Thrall's right. He turned to see Doomhammer, his black plate armor shiny with what could only be spilled human blood. "Success! You are free, my brethren. You are free!"

And the cry that swelled up into the moonless night filled Thrall's heart with joy.

* * *

"If you bear the news I think you do, then I am inclined to separate your pretty head from your shoulders," Blackmoore growled at the hapless messenger who wore a baldric that marked him as a rider from one of the internment camps.

The messenger looked slightly ill. "Perhaps, then, I ought not speak," he replied.

There was a bottle to Blackmoore's right that seemed to keep calling to him. He ignored its song, though his palms were sweaty.

"Let me guess. There has been another uprising at one of the encampments. All of the orcs have escaped. No one knows where they are."

"Lord Blackmoore," stammered the young messenger, "will you still cut my head off if I confirm your words?"

Anger exploded through Blackmoore so sharply it was almost a physical pain. Hard on that passionate emotion was a profound sense of black despair. What was going on? How could those cattle, those sheep in orc guise, rally themselves sufficiently to overthrow their captors? Who were these orcs who had come out of nowhere, armed to the teeth and as full of hatred and fury as they had been two decades past? There were rumors that Doomhammer, curse his rotten soul, had come out of hiding and was leading these incursions. One guard had sworn that he had seen the black plate that bastard was famous for wearing.

"You may keep your head," said Blackmoore,

acutely aware of the bottle that was within arm's reach. "But only that you may carry a message back to your superiors."

"Sir," said the messenger miserably, "there's more."

Blackmoore peered up at him with bloodshot eyes. "How much more can there possibly be?"

"This time, the instigator was positively identified. It was—"

"Doomhammer, yes, I've heard the rumors."

"No, my lord." The messenger swallowed. Blackmoore could actually see sweat popping out on the youth's brow. "The leader of these rebellions is . . . is Thrall, my lord."

Blackmoore felt the blood drain from his face. "You're a damned liar, my man," he said, softly. "Or at least you'd better tell me you are."

"Nay, my lord, though I would it were not so. My master said he fought him in hand-to-hand combat, and remembered Thrall from the gladiator battles."

"I'll have your master's tongue for telling such untruths!" bellowed Blackmoore.

"Alas, sir, you'll have to dig six feet to get his tongue," said the messenger. "He died only an hour after the battle."

Overcome with this new information, Blackmoore sank back in his chair and tried to compose his thoughts. A quick drink would help, but he knew that he was drinking too much in front of people. He was starting to hear the whispers: *drunken fool . . . who's in command here now . . . .*

No. He licked his lips. *I'm Aedelas Blackmoore, Lord of Durnholde, master of the encampments . . . I trained that green-skinned, black-blooded freak, I ought to be able to out-think him . . . by the Light, just one drink to steady these hands. . . .*

A strange feeling of pride stole through him. He'd been right about Thrall's potential all along. He knew he'd been something special, something more than just an ordinary orc. If only Thrall hadn't spurned the chances Blackmoore had given him! They could be leading the charge against the Alliance even now, with Blackmoore riding at the head of a loyal gathering of orcs, obedient to his every command. Foolish, foolish Thrall. For the briefest of moments, Blackmoore's thoughts drifted back toward that final beating he had given Thrall. Perhaps that had been a bit much.

But he would not let himself feel guilt, not over his treatment of a disobedient slave. Thrall had thrown it all away to ally with these grunting, stinking, worthless thugs. Let him rot where he would fall.

His attention returned to the trembling messenger, and Blackmoore forced a smile. The man relaxed, smiling tentatively back. With an unsteady hand, Blackmoore reached for a quill, dipped it in ink, and began to write a message. He powdered it to absorb the excess ink and gave it a few moments to dry. Then he carefully folded the missive into thirds, dripped hot wax on it, and set his seal.

Handing it to the messenger, he said, "Take this to your master. And have a care for that neck of yours, young sir."

Apparently having difficulty believing his good fortune, the messenger bowed deeply and hurried out, probably before Blackmoore could change his mind. Alone, Blackmoore lunged for the bottle, uncorked it, and took several long, deep pulls. As he lowered the bottle from his lips, it spilled on his black doublet. He wiped at the stains, disinterested. That's what he had servants for.

"Tammis!" he yelled. At once the door opened and the servant stuck his head in.

"Yes, sir?"

"Go find Langston." He smiled. "I've got a task for him to complete."

SIXTEEN

Thrall had successfully managed to infiltrate and liberate three encampments. After the first, of course, security had been stepped up at the encampments. It was still pathetically lax, and the men who "captured" Thrall never seemed to expect him to stir up trouble.

But during the battle for the third, he had been recognized. The element of surprise had now vanished, and after talking with Hellscream and Doomhammer, it was decided that it would be too risky for Thrall to continue to pose as just another prisoner.

"It is your spirit, my friend, that has roused us. You cannot continue to put yourself into such jeopardy," said Hellscream. His eyes blazed with what Thrall now knew to be demonic hellfire.

"I cannot sit safely behind our lines, letting everyone else face the danger while I shirk it," Thrall replied.

"We are not suggesting that," said Doomhammer. "But the tactic we have utilized has now become too dangerous."

"Humans talk," said Thrall, recalling all the rumors and stories he had heard while training. The human trainees had thought him too stupid to comprehend, and had spoken freely in his presence. The thought still rankled, but he had welcomed the knowledge. "The orcs in the prisons cannot help but overhear how the other camps have been freed. Even if they do not care to listen, they will know that something is afoot. Even if I am not there physically to tell them of the way of the shaman, we can hope that somehow our message has gotten through. Once the way is clear, let us hope they will find their own paths to freedom."

And so it had been. The fourth camp had been bristling with armed guards, but the elements continued to come to Thrall's aid when he asked it of them. This further convinced him that his cause was right and just, for otherwise, the spirits would surely decline their help. It had been harder to destroy the walls and fight the guards, and many of Doomhammer's finest warriors had lost their lives. But the orcs imprisoned within those cold stone walls had eagerly responded, flowing through the breach almost before Doomhammer and his warriors were ready for them.

The new Horde grew almost daily. Hunting was

easy at this time of year, and Doomhammer's followers did not go hungry. When he heard of a small group taking it upon themselves to storm an outlying town, Thrall was furious. Especially when he learned that many unarmed humans had been killed.

He learned who the leader of the excursion was, and that night he marched into that group's encampment, seized the startled orc, and slammed him hard into the ground.

"We are not butchers of humans!" Thrall cried. "We fight to free our imprisoned brothers, and our opponents are armed soldiers, not milkmaids and children!"

The orc started to protest, and Thrall backhanded him savagely. The orc's head jerked to the side and blood spilled from his mouth.

"The forest teems with deer and hare! Every camp we liberate provides us with food! There is no call to terrorize people who have offered us no harm simply for our amusement. You fight where I tell you to fight, who I tell you to fight, and if any orc ever again offers harm to an unarmed human, I will not forgive it. Is this understood?"

The orc nodded. Everyone around his campfire stared at Thrall with huge eyes and nodded as well.

Thrall softened a bit. "Such behavior is of the old Horde, led by dark warlocks who had no love for our people. That is what brought us to the internment camps, to the listlessness caused by the lack of demon energy upon which we fed so greedily. I do not wish us beholden to anyone but ourselves. That way almost destroyed us. We will be free, never question that. But we will be free to be who we truly are, and who we truly are is much, much more than simply a race of beings who exist to slaughter humans. The old ways are no more. We fight as proud warriors now, not as indiscriminate killers. There is no pride in murdering children."

He turned and left. Stunned silence followed him. He heard a rumble of laughter in the dark, and turned to see Doomhammer. "You walk the hard path," the great Warchief said. "It is in their blood to kill."

"I do not believe that," said Thrall. "I believe that we were corrupted from noble warriors into assassins. Puppets, whose strings were pulled by demons and those of our own people who betrayed us."

"It . . . is a dreadful dance," came Hellscream's voice, so soft and weak that Thrall almost didn't recognize it. "To be used so. The power they give . . . it is like the sweetest honey, the juiciest flesh. You are fortunate never to have drunk from that well, Thrall. And then to be without it, it is almost . . . unbearable." He shuddered.

Thrall placed a hand on Hellscream's shoulder. "And yet, you have borne it, brave one," he said. "You make my courage as nothing with yours."

Hellscream's red eyes glowed in the darkness, and by their hellish crimson light, Thrall could see him smile.

* * *

It was in the small, dark hours of the morning when the new Horde, led by Doomhammer, Hellscream, and Thrall, surrounded the fifth encampment.

The outriders returned. "The guards are alert," they told Doomhammer. "There is double the usual number posted on the walls. They have lit many fires so that their weak eyes can see."

"And it is full moons' light," said Doomhammer, glancing up at the glowing silver and blue-green orbs. "The White Lady and the Blue Child are not our friends tonight."

"We cannot wait two more weeks," said Hellscream. "The Horde is eager for a just battle, and we must strike while they are still strong enough to resist the demon listlessness."

Doomhammer nodded, though he still looked concerned. To the scouts, he said, "Any sign that they are expecting an assault?" One of these days, Thrall knew, their luck would run out. They had been very careful not to select camps in any particular order, so that the humans would not be able to guess where they would strike next and thus could not be lying in wait. But Thrall knew Blackmoore, and knew that somehow, some way, a confrontation was inevitable.

While he relished the thought of finally facing Blackmoore in fair combat, he knew what it would mean to the troops. For their sake, he hoped that tonight was not that night.

The outriders shook their heads.

"Then let us descend," said Doomhammer, and in steady silence, the green tide flooded down the hill and toward the encampment.

They had almost reached it when the gates flew open and dozens of armed, mounted humans charged out. Thrall saw the black falcon on the red and gold standard, and knew that the day he had both dreaded and anticipated had finally arrived.

Hellscream's battle cry pierced the air, almost drowning out the screams of humans and the pounding of their horses' hooves. Rather than being disheartened by the enemy's strength, the Horde seemed revitalized, willing to rise to the challenge.

Thrall threw back his head and howled his own battle cry. The quarters were too close for Thrall to call on such great powers as lightning and earthquakes, but there were others he could ask to aid him. Despite an almost overwhelming desire to charge into the fray and fight hand to hand, he held back. Time enough for that once he had done all he could to tip the balance in the orcs' direction.

He closed his eyes, planted his feet firmly on the grass, and sought the Spirit of the Wilds. He saw in his mind's eye a great white horse, the Spirit of all horses, and sent forth his plea.

The humans are using your children to kill us. They, too, are in danger. If the horses throw their riders, they will be free to reach safety. Will you ask them to do so?

The great horse considered. *These children are trained to fight. They are not afraid of swords and spears.*

But there is no need for them to die today. We are only trying to free our people. That is a just cause, and not worth their deaths.

Again, the great horse spirit considered Thrall's words. Finally, he nodded his enormous white head.

Suddenly, the battlefield was thrown into greater confusion as every horse either wheeled and galloped off, bearing a startled and furious human with it, or began to rear and buck. The human guards fought to stay mounted, but it was impossible.

Now it was time to beseech the Spirit of Earth. Thrall envisioned the roots of the forest that surrounded the camp extending, growing, exploding up from the soil. *Trees who have sheltered us . . . will you aid me now?*

Yes, came a response in his mind. Thrall opened his eyes and strained to see. Even with his superb night vision, it was hard to discern what was happening, but he could just make it out.

Roots exploded from the hard-packed earth just outside the camp walls. They shot up from the soil and seized the men who had been dismounted, wrapping their pale lengths about the humans as firmly as the trap-nets closed about captive orcs. To Thrall's approval, the orcs did not kill the fallen guards as they lay helpless. Instead they ran on to other targets, pressed inward, and searched for their imprisoned kin.

Another wave of enemies charged out, this one on foot. The trees did not send their roots forth a second time; they had provided all the aid they would. Despite his frustration, Thrall thanked them and racked his brain as to what to do next.

He decided that he had done all he could as a shaman. It was time for him to behave as a warrior. Gripping his mammoth broadsword, a gift from Hellscream, Thrall charged down the hill to aid his brothers.

Lord Karramyn Langston had never been more afraid in his life.

Too young to have charged into battle in the last conflict between humankind and orcs, he had hung on every word his idol Lord Blackmoore had uttered. Blackmoore had made it sound as easy as hunting game in the tame, forested lands that surrounded Durnholde, except much more exciting. Blackmoore had said nothing about the shrieks and groans that assaulted his ears, the stench of blood and urine and feces and the orcs themselves, the bombardment of a thousand images upon the eye at any one time. No, battle with orcs had been described as a heart-pounding lark, which made one ready for a bath and wine and the company of adoring women.

They had had the element of surprise. They had been ready for the green monsters. What had happened? Why had the horses, well-trained beasts every one of them, fled or bucked off their riders? What wicked sorcery made the earth shoot up pale arms to bind those unfortunate enough to fall? Where were the horrible white wolves coming from, and how did they know whom to attack?

Langston got none of these questions answered. He was ostensibly in command of the unit, but any semblance of control he might have had dissolved once those terrifying tendrils emerged from the earth. Now there was only sheer panic, the sound of sword on shield or flesh, and the cries of the dying.

He himself didn't know whom he was fighting. It was too dark to see, and he swung his sword blindly, crying and sobbing with every wild strike. Sometimes Langston's sword bit into flesh, but most of the time he heard it cutting only the air. He was fueled by the energy of sheer terror, and a distant part of him marveled at his ability to keep swinging.

A solid, strong blow on his shield jangled his arm all the way to his teeth. Somehow, he kept it lifted under the onslaught of a creature that was hugely tall and enormously strong. For a fleeting second, Langston's eyes met those of his attacker and his mouth dropped open in shock.

"Thrall!" he cried.

The orc's eyes widened in recognition, then narrowed in fury. Langston saw a mammoth green fist rise up, and then he knew no more.

Thrall did not care about the lives of Langston's men. They stood between him and the liberation of the imprisoned orcs. They had come openly into honest combat and if they died, then that was their destiny. But Langston, he wanted kept alive.

He remembered Blackmoore's little shadow. Langston never said much, just looked upon Blackmoore with a fawning expression and upon Thrall with loathing and contempt. But Thrall knew that no one was closer to his enemy than this pathetic, weak-willed man, and though he did not deserve it, Thrall was going to see to it that Langston survived this battle.

He flung the unconscious captain over his shoulder and fought his way back against the pressing tide of continued battle. Hurrying back up to the shelter of the forest, he tossed Langston down at the foot of an ancient oak as if he were no more than a sack of potatoes. He tied the man's hands with his own baldric. *Guard him well until I return,* he told the old oak. In answer, the mammoth roots lifted and folded themselves none too gently about Langston's prone form.

Thrall turned and raced back down toward the battle. Usually the liberations were accomplished with astonishing speed, but not this time. The fighting was still continuing when Thrall rejoined his comrades, and it seemed to last forever. But the imprisoned orcs were doing everything they could to scramble toward freedom. At one point, Thrall fought his way past the humans and began searching the encampment. He found several still cowering in corners. They shrank from him at first, and with his blood so hot from battle it was difficult for Thrall to speak gently to them. Nonetheless, he managed to coax each group into coming with him, into making the desperate dash for freedom past groups of clustered, fighting warriors.

Finally, when he was certain that all the inhabitants had fled, he returned to the thick of the fray himself. He looked around. There was Hellscream, fighting with all the power and passion of a demon himself. But where was Doomhammer? Usually the charismatic Warchief had called for retreat by this time, so the orcs could regroup, tend to their wounded, and plan for the next assault.

It was a bloody battle, and too many of his brothers and sisters in arms already lay dead or dying. Thrall, as second in command, took it upon himself to cry, "Retreat! Retreat!"

Lost in the bloodlust, many did not hear him. Thrall raced from warrior to warrior, fending off attacks, screaming the word the orcs never liked to hear but was necessary, even vital, to their continued existence. "Retreat! *Retreat!*"

His screams penetrated the haze of battlelust at last, and with a few final blows, the orcs turned and moved purposefully out of the confines of the encampment. Many of the human knights, for knights it was clear they were, gave chase. Thrall waited outside, crying, "Go, go!" The orcs were larger, stronger, and faster than the humans, and when the last one was sprinting up the hill toward freedom, Thrall whirled, planted his feet in the foul-smelling mud that was hard earth and blood commingled, and called on the Spirit of Earth at last.

The earth responded. The ground beneath the encampment began to tremble, and small shocks rippled out from the center. Before Thrall's eyes, earth broke and heaved, the mighty stone wall encircling the camp shattering and falling into small pieces. Screams assaulted Thrall's ears, not battle cries or epithets, but cries of genuine terror. He steeled himself against a quick rush of pity. These knights came at the order of Blackmoore. More than likely they had been instructed to slay as many orcs as possible, imprison all they did not slay, and capture Thrall in order to return him to a life of slavery. They had chosen to follow those orders, and for that, they would pay with their lives.

The earth buckled. The screaming was drowned out by the terrible roar of collapsing buildings and shattering stone. And then, almost as quickly as it had come, the noises ceased.

Thrall stood and regarded the rubble that had once been an internment camp for his people. A few soft moans came from under the debris, but Thrall hardened his heart. His own people were wounded, were moaning. He would tend to them.

He took a moment to close his eyes and offer his

gratitude to Earth, then turned and hastened to where his people were gathering.

This moment was always chaotic, but it seemed to Thrall to be even less organized than usual. Even as he ran up the hilly ground, Hellscream was hurrying to meet him.

"It's Doomhammer," Hellscream rasped. "You had better hurry."

Thrall's heart leaped. Not Doomhammer. Surely he could not be in danger. . . . He followed where Hellscream led, shoving his way through a thick cluster of jabbering orcs to where Orgrim Doomhammer lay propped up sideways against the base of a tree.

Thrall gasped, horrified. At least two feet of a broken lance extended from Doomhammer's broad back. As Thrall stared, frozen for a moment by the sight, Doomhammer's two personal attendants struggled to remove the circular breastplate. Now Thrall could see, poking through the black gambeson that cushioned the heavy armor, the reddened, glistening tip of the lance. It had impaled Doomhammer with such force that it had gone clear through his body, completely piercing the back plate and denting the breastplate from the inside.

Drek'Thar was kneeling next to Doomhammer, and he turned his blind eyes up to Thrall's. He shook his head slightly, then rose and stepped back.

Blood seemed to roar in Thrall's ears, and it was only dimly that he heard the mighty warrior calling his name. Stumbling in shock, Thrall approached and knelt beside Doomhammer.

"The blow was a coward's blow," Doomhammer rasped. Blood trickled from his mouth. "I was struck from behind."

"My lord," said Thrall, miserably. Doomhammer waved him to silence.

"I need your help, Thrall. In two things. You must carry on what we have begun. I led the Horde once. It is not my destiny to do so again." He grimaced, shuddered, and continued. "Yours is the title of Warchief, Thrall, son of D-Durotan. You will wear my armor, and carry my hammer."

Doomhammer reached out to Thrall, and Thrall grasped the bloody, armored hand with his own. "You know what to do. They are in your care now. I could not . . . have hoped for a better heir. Your father would be so proud . . . help me. . . ."

With hands that trembled, Thrall turned to assist the two younger orcs in removing, piece by piece, the armor that had always been associated with Orgrim Doomhammer. But the lance that still protruded from Orgrim's back would not permit the removal of the rest of the armor.

"That is the second thing," growled Doomhammer. There was a small crowd clustered around the fallen hero, and more were coming up every moment. "It is shame enough that I die from a coward's strike," he said. "I will not leave my life with this piece of human treachery still in my body." One hand went to the point of the lance. The fingers fluttered weakly, and the hand fell. "I have tried to pull it out myself, but I lack the strength. . . . Hurry, Thrall. Do this for me."

Thrall felt as though his chest were being crushed by an unseen hand. He nodded. Steeling himself against the pain that he knew he would need to cause his friend and mentor, he closed his armored fingers about the tip, pressing into Doomhammer's flesh.

Doomhammer cried out, in anger as much as in pain. "Pull!" he cried.

Closing his eyes, Thrall pulled. The blood-soaked shaft came forward a few inches. The sound that Doomhammer made almost broke Thrall's heart.

"Again!" the mighty warrior cried. Thrall took a deep breath and pulled, willing himself to remove the entire shaft this time. It came free with such suddenness that he stumbled backward.

Black-red blood now gushed freely from the fatal hole in Doomhammer's belly. Standing beside Thrall, Hellscream whispered, "I saw it happen. It was before you caused the horses to desert their masters. He was single-handedly battling eight of them, all on horseback. It was the bravest thing I have ever seen."

Thrall nodded dumbly, then knelt beside Doomhammer's side. "Great leader," whispered Thrall, so that only Doomhammer could hear, "I am afraid. I am not worthy to wear your armor and wield your weapon."

"No one breathes who is worthier," said Doomhammer in a soft, wet voice. "You will lead them . . . to victory . . . and you will lead them . . . to peace. . . ."

The eyes closed, and Doomhammer fell forward onto Thrall. Thrall caught him, and held him close for a long moment. He felt a hand on his shoulder. It was Drek'Thar, who slipped a hand beneath Thrall's arm and helped him rise.

"They are watching," Drek'Thar said to Thrall, speaking very softly. "They must not lose heart. You must put on the armor at once, and show them that they have a new chieftain."

"Sir," said one of the orcs who had overheard Drek'Thar's words, "the armor. . . ." He swallowed. "The plate that was pierced—it will need to be replaced."

"No," said Thrall. "It will not. Before the next battle you will hammer it back into shape, but I will keep the plate. In honor of Orgrim Doomhammer, who gave his life to free his people."

He stood and let them place the armor on, grieving privately but publicly showing a brave face. The gathered crowd watched, hushed and reverent. Drek'Thar's advice had been sound; this was the right thing to do. He bent, picked up the enormous hammer, and swung it over his head.

"Orgrim Doomhammer has named me Warchief," he cried. "It is a title I would not have sought, but I have no choice. I have been named, and so I will obey. Who will follow me to lead our people to freedom?"

A cry rose up, raw and filled with grief for the passing of their leader. Yet it was a sound of hope as well, and as Thrall stood, bearing aloft the famous weapon of Doomhammer, he knew in his heart that, despite the odds, victory would indeed be theirs.

SEVENTEEN

It was raw with grief and fueled by anger that Thrall marched up to where Langston fought against the implacable tree roots in a desperate attempt to sit up.

He shrank back when Thrall arrived, wearing the legendary black plate mail and towering over him. His eyes were wide with fear.

"I should kill you," said Thrall, darkly. The image of Doomhammer dying in front of his eyes was still fresh in his mind.

Langston licked his red, full lips. "Mercy, Lord Thrall," he begged.

Thrall dropped to one knee and shoved his face within inches of Langston's. "And when did you show me mercy?" he roared. Langston winced at the sound. "When did you intervene to say, 'Blackmoore, perhaps you've beaten him enough,' or 'Blackmoore, he did the best he could'? When did such words ever cross your lips?"

"I wanted to," said Langston.

"Right now you believe those words," said Thrall, rising again to his full height and staring down at his captive. "But I have no doubt that you never truly felt that way. Let us dispense with lies. Your life has value to me—for the moment. If you tell me what I want to know, I will release you and the other prisoners and let you return to your dog of a master." Langston looked doubtful. "You have my word," Thrall added.

"Of what worth is the word of an orc?" Langston said, rallying for a moment.

"Why, it's worth your pathetic life, Langston. Though I'll grant you, that is not worth much. Now, tell me. How did you know which camp we would be attacking? Is there a spy in our midst?"

Langston looked like a sullen child and refused to answer. Thrall formed a thought, and the tree roots tightened about Langston's body. He gasped and stared up at Thrall in shock.

"Yes," said Thrall, "the very trees obey my command. As do all the elements." Langston didn't need to know about the give-and-take relationship a shaman had with the spirits. Let him assume Thrall had complete control. "Answer my question."

"No spy," grunted Langston. He was having difficulty breathing due to the root across his chest. Thrall asked that it be loosened, and the tree complied.

"Blackmoore has put a group of knights at all the remaining camps."

"So that no matter where we struck, we would encounter his men." Langston nodded. "Hardly a good use of resources, but it appears to have worked this time. What else can you tell me? What is Blackmoore doing to ensure my recovery? How many troops does he have? Or will that root creep up to your throat?"

The root in question gently stroked Langston's neck. Langston's resistance shattered like a glass goblet dropped on a stone floor. Tears welled up in his eyes and he began to sob. Thrall was disgusted, but not enough that he didn't pay close attention to Langston's words. The knight blurted out numbers, dates, plans, even the fact that Blackmoore's drinking was beginning to affect his judgment.

"He desperately wants you back, Thrall," snuffled Langston, peering up at Thrall with red-rimmed eyes. "You were the key to everything."

Instantly alert, Thrall demanded, "Explain." As the confining roots fell away from his body, Langston appeared heartened, and even more eager to tell everything he knew.

"The key to everything," he repeated. "When he found you, he knew that he could use you. First as a gladiator, but as so much more than that." He wiped his wet face and tried to recover as much of his lost dignity as he could. "Didn't you wonder why he taught you how to read? Gave you maps, taught you Hawks and Hares and strategy?"

Thrall nodded, tense and expectant.

"It was because he eventually wanted you to lead an army. An army of orcs."

Anger flooded Thrall. "You are lying. Why would Blackmoore want me to lead his rivals?"

"But they—you—wouldn't be rivals," said Langston. "You would lead an army of orcs against the Alliance."

Thrall gaped. He couldn't believe what he was hearing. He had known Blackmoore was a cruel, conniving bastard, but this . . . It was treachery on a staggering level, against his own kind! Surely this was a lie. But Langston appeared to be in dire earnest, and once the shock had worn off, Thrall realized that to Blackmoore it would make a great deal of sense.

"You were the best of both worlds," Langston continued. "The power and strength and bloodlust of an orc, combined with the intelligence and strategic knowledge of a human. You would command the orcs and they would be invincible."

"And Aedelas Blackmoore would be Lieutenant General no longer, but . . . what? King? Absolute monarch? Lord of all?"

Langston nodded furiously. "You can't imagine what he's been like since you escaped. It's been hard on all of us."

"Hard?" snarled Thrall. "I was beaten and kicked and made to think that I was less than nothing! I faced death nearly every day in the arena. I and my people are battling for our very lives. We are fighting for freedom. *That*, Langston, that is hard. Do not speak to me of pain and difficulty, for you have known precious little of either."

Langston fell silent and Thrall pondered what he had just learned. It was a bold and audacious strategy, but then again, whatever his many faults, Aedelas Blackmoore was a bold and audacious man. Thrall had learned a little, here and there, about the Blackmoore family's disgrace. Aedelas had always been eager to wipe the blot from his name, but perhaps the stain went deep. Perhaps it went all the way to the bone—or to the heart.

Why, though, if Blackmoore's aim had ultimately been to win Thrall's complete loyalty, had he not been treated better? Memories floated into Thrall's mind that he had not recalled in years: an amusing game of Hawks and Hares with a laughing Blackmoore; a plateful of sweets sent down from the kitchens after a particularly fine battle; an affectionate hand placed on a huge shoulder when Thrall had conquered a particularly tricky strategic problem.

Blackmoore had always aroused many feelings in Thrall. Fear, adoration, hatred, contempt. But for the first time, Thrall realized that, in many ways, Blackmoore deserved his pity. At the time, Thrall had not known why it was that sometimes Blackmoore was open and jovial, his voice clipped and erudite, and sometimes he was brutal and nasty, his voice slurred and unnaturally loud. Now, he understood; the bottle had gotten its talons as firmly into Blackmoore as an eagle's sank into a hare. Blackmoore was a man torn between embracing a legacy of treachery and overcoming it, of being a brilliant strategist and fighter and being a cowardly, vicious bully. Blackmoore had probably treated Thrall as well as he knew how.

The rage left Thrall. He felt terribly sorry for Blackmoore but the feeling changed nothing. He still was driven to liberate the encampments, and aid the orcs in rediscovering the power of their heritage. Blackmoore stood in the way, an obstacle that would need to be eliminated.

He looked back down at Langston, who sensed the change in him and gave him a smile that looked more like a grimace.

"I keep my word," Thrall said. "You and your men will go free. You will leave, now. With no weapons, no food, no mounts. You will be followed, but you will not see who follows you; and if you speak of an ambush, or attempt any kind of attack, you will die. Is this understood?"

Langston nodded. With a jerk of his head, Thrall indicated that he could leave. Langston needed no second urging. He scrambled to his feet and bolted. Thrall watched him and the other disarmed knights fleeing into the darkness. He looked up into the trees and saw the owl he had sensed staring back down at him with lambent eyes. The night bird hooted softly.

Follow them, my friend, if you will. Report back to me at once if they plan action against us.

With a rustle of wings, the owl sprang from the branch and began to follow the fleeing men. Thrall sighed deeply. Now that the keyed-up energy that had supported him through this long, bloody night was fading, he realized that he himself had suffered injuries and was exhausted. But these things could be tended to later. There was a more important duty to perform.

It took the rest of the night to gather and prepare the bodies, and by morning, black smoke was curling thickly into the blue skies. Thrall and Drek'Thar had asked the Spirit of Fire to burn more quickly than was its usual wont, so it would not take nearly as long for the bodies to be reduced to ashes, and those ashes given to Spirit of Air to scatter as it saw fit.

The largest and most decorated pyre was reserved for the most noble of them all. It took Thrall, Hellscream, and two others to lift Orgrim Doomhammer's massive corpse onto the pyre. Reverently, Drek'Thar anointed Doomhammer's nearly naked body with oils, murmuring words that Thrall could not hear. Sweet scents rose up from the body. Drek'Thar indicated that Thrall join him, and together they posed the body in an attitude of defiance. Dead fingers were folded and discreetly tied about a ruined sword. At Doomhammer's feet were laid the corpses of other brave warriors who had died in battle—the fierce, loyal white wolves who had not been swift enough to elude the humans' weapons. One lay at Doomhammer's feet, two more on each side, and across his chest, in a place of honor, was the grizzled, courageous Wise-ear. Drek'Thar patted his old friend one last time, then he and Thrall stepped back.

Thrall expected Drek'Thar to say whatever words might be appropriate, but instead Hellscream nudged Thrall. Uncertainly, Thrall addressed the crowd who gathered, hushed, about their former chieftain's corpse.

"I have not been long in the company of my own people," Thrall began. "I do not know the traditions of the afterlife. But this I know: Doomhammer died as bravely as it is possible for any orc to die. He fought in battle, trying to liberate his imprisoned kin. Surely, he will regard us with favor, as we honor him now in death as we all honored him in life." He looked over at the dead orc's face. "Orgrim Doomhammer, you were my father's best friend. I could not hope to know a nobler being. Speed to whatever joyous place and purpose await you."

With that, he closed his eyes and asked the Spirit of Fire to take the hero. Immediately, the fire burnt more swiftly and with more heat than Thrall had ever experienced. The body would soon be consumed, and the shell that had housed the fiery spirit called in this world Orgrim Doomhammer would soon be no more.

But what he had stood for, what he had died for, would never be forgotten.

Thrall tilted his head back and bellowed a deep cry.

One by one, others joined him, screaming their pain and passion. If there were indeed ancestral spirits, even they must have been impressed by the volume of the lamentation raised for Orgrim Doomhammer.

Once the rite was done, Thrall sat heavily down beside Drek'Thar and Hellscream. Hellscream, too, had suffered injuries which he, like Thrall, simply chose to bear stoically for the moment. Drek'Thar had been expressly forbidden to be anywhere near the fighting, though he served loyally and well by tending to the injured. If anything happened to Thrall, Drek'Thar was the only shaman among them, and far too precious a resource to risk losing. He was not yet so old that the order didn't vex him, however.

"What encampment is next, my Warchief?" said Hellscream respectfully. Thrall winced at the term. He was still getting used to the fact that Doomhammer was gone, that he was now in charge of hundreds of orcs.

"No more encampments," he said. "Our force is large enough for the present moment."

Drek'Thar frowned. "They suffer," he said.

"They do," Thrall agreed, "but I have a plan to liberate all of them at once. To kill the monster, you must cut off his head, not just his hands and feet. It is time to cut off the head of the internment camp system."

His eyes glittered in the firelight. "We will storm Durnholde."

* * *

The next morning, when he announced the plan to the troops, huge cheers greeted him. They were ready, now, to tackle the seat of power. Thrall and Drek'Thar had the elements standing ready to aid them. The orcs were only revitalized by the battle of last night; few of them had fallen, though one was the greatest warrior of them all, and many of the enemy now lay dead around the blasted remains of the encampment. The ravens who circled were grateful for the feast.

They were several days' march away, but food was plentiful and spirits were high. By the time the sun was fully in the sky, the orcish Horde, under their new leader Thrall, was moving steadily and purposefully toward Durnholde.

"Of course I told him nothing," said Langston, sipping Blackmoore's wine. "He captured and tortured me, but I held my tongue, I tell you. Out of admiration, he let me and my men go."

Privately, Blackmoore doubted this, but said nothing. "Tell me more about these feats he performs," he asked.

Happy to regain his mentor's approval, Langston launched into a fabulous tale about roots clutching his body, lightning striking on command, well-trained horses abandoning their masters, and the very earth shattering a stone enclosure. If Blackmoore hadn't heard similar stories from the few men who returned, he would have been inclined to think that Langston had been hitting the bottle even harder than he.

"I was on the right path," Blackmoore mused, taking another gulp of wine. "In capturing Thrall. You see what he is, what he has done with that pathetic bunch of slumping, disheartened greenskins."

It was physically painful to think that he had come so close to manipulating this clearly powerful new Horde. Hard on the heels of that came a mental image of Taretha, and her letters of friendship to his slave. As always, anger mixed with a strange, sharp pain rose in him at the thought. He had let her be, never let her know that he had found the letters. He hadn't even let Langston know about that, and was now profoundly grateful for his wisdom. He believed that Langston had probably babbled everything he knew to Thrall, which necessitated a change of plan.

"I fear others were likely not as staunch as you in the face of torture by orcs, my friend," he said, trying and failing to keep the sarcasm out of his voice. Fortunately, Langston was so far in his cups that he didn't appear to notice. "We must assume that the orcs know all that we know, and act accordingly. We must try to think like Thrall. What would be his next move? What is his ultimate goal?"

And how in all the hells there are can I find a way to reclaim him?

Though he was leading an army of nearly two thousand, and it was almost certain to be spotted, Thrall did what he could to disguise the march of the Horde. He asked the earth to cover their prints, the air to carry their scent away from any beasts who might sound the alert. It was little, but every bit helped.

He made the encampment several miles south of Durnholde, in a wild and generally avoided forested area. Together with a small group of scouts, he set off for a certain wooded area directly outside the fortress. Both Hellscream and Drek'Thar had tried to dissuade him, but he insisted.

"I have a plan," he said, "one that may achieve our goals without undue bloodshed from either side."

EIGHTEEN

E ven on the coldest days of winter, save when there was an active blizzard preventing any-one departing Durnholde, Taretha had gone to visit the lightning-felled tree. And each time she peered into the tree's black depths, she saw nothing.

She enjoyed the return of warmer weather, though the snowmelt-saturated earth sucked on her boots and more than once succeeded in pulling one off. Having to tug her boot free and put it on a second time was a trivial price to pay for the fresh smells of the awakening woods, the shafts of sunlight piercing the darkness of the shadows, and the astounding blaze of color that dotted the meadows and forest floor alike.

Thrall's exploits had been the talk of Durnholde. The conversations served only to increase Black-moore's drinking. Which, at times, was not a bad thing. More than once she had arrived at his bedchamber and entered quietly, to find the Master of Durnholde asleep on floor, chair, or bed, a bottle somewhere nearby. On those nights, Taretha Foxton breathed a sigh of relief, closed the door, and slept alone in her own small room.

A few days ago, young Lord Langston had returned, with tales that sounded too preposterous to frighten a child still in the nursery. And yet . . . hadn't she read of ancient powers the orcs had once possessed? Powers in harmony with nature, long ago? She knew that Thrall was profoundly intelligent, and it would not at all surprise her to discover that he had learned these ancient arts.

Taretha was approaching the old tree now, and looked into its depths with a casualness born of repetition.

And gasped. Her hand flew to her mouth as her heart began to pound so fiercely she feared she would faint. There, nestled in a brown-black hollow, was her necklace. It seemed to catch the sunlight and glow like a silver beacon to her. With trembling fingers, she reached for it, grasped it, and then dropped it.

"Clumsy!" she hissed, picking it up again with a slightly steadier hand.

It could be a trick. Thrall could have been captured and the necklace taken from him. It might even have been recognized as hers. But unless Thrall told someone about their compact, who would know to leave it here? She was certain of one thing: Nobody could break Thrall.

Tears of joy filled her eyes and spilled down her cheeks. She wiped at them with the back of her left hand, the right one still cradling the crescent pendant.

He was here, in these woods, likely hiding in the dragonlike cliffside. He was waiting for her to help him. Perhaps he was injured. Her hands folded over the necklace and she tucked it inside her dress, carefully out of sight. It would be best if no one saw her "missing" necklace.

Happier than she had been since she had last seen the orc, and yet filled with worry for his safety, Taretha returned to Durnholde.

The day seemed to last forever. She was grateful that the dinner tonight was fish; more than once, she'd gotten ill on poorly prepared fish. The chef at Durnholde had served with Blackmoore in battle over twenty years ago. He had been hired as a reward for his service, not for his cooking.

Of course, she did not eat at the table in the great hall with Blackmoore. He would not dream of having a servant girl sit beside him in front of his noble friends. *Good enough to bed, not good enough to wed,* she thought, recalling the old childhood verse. All the better tonight.

"You seem a bit preoccupied, my dear," Tammis said to his daughter as they sat together at the small table in their quarters. "Are you . . . well?"

The slightly strained tone of his voice and the frightened look her mother gave Taretha at the question almost made her smile. They were worried that she was pregnant. That would help with her deception tonight.

"Very well, Da," she answered, folding her hand over his. "But this fish . . . does it taste all right to you?"

Clannia prodded her own fish in cream sauce with her two-pronged fork. "It tastes well enough, for being Randrel's cooking."

In truth, the fish was fairly tasty. Still, Taretha took another bite, chewed, swallowed, and made a slight face. She made a bit of a show of pushing the plate away from her. As her father peeled an orange, Taretha closed her eyes and whimpered.

"I'm sorry. . . ." She rushed out of the room to her own quarters, making noises as if she was about to be sick. She reached her room, on the same floor as her parents', and made loud noises over the chamber pot. She had to smile a little; it would be amusing, were the stakes not so high.

There came an urgent knock on the door. "Darling, it's me," called Clannia. She opened the door. Taretha put the empty chamber pot out of sight. "Poor dear. You look pale as milk."

That, at least, Taretha didn't have to feign. "Please . . . can Da have a word with the Master? I don't think. . . ."

Clannia colored bright pink. Although everyone knew that Taretha had become Blackmoore's mistress, no one spoke of it. "Certainly, my dear, certainly. Would you like to stay with us tonight?"

"No," she said, quickly. "No, I'm fine. I'd just like to be alone for a bit." She lifted her hand to her mouth again, and Clannia nodded.

"As you will, Tari dear. Good night. Let us know if you need anything."

Her mother closed the door behind her, and Taretha let out a long, deep breath. Now, to wait until it was safe to leave. She was next to the kitchens, one of the last places that settled down for the night. When all was still, she ventured forth. First, she went to the kitchens, placing as much food as she could lay her hands on into the sack. Earlier today, she had torn up some old dresses for bandages, should Thrall need them.

Blackmoore's habits were as predictable as the sun's rising and setting. If he started drinking at dinner, as was his wont, he would be ready to entertain her in his bedchamber by the time dinner was over. Afterward, he would fall into a slumber, almost a stupor, and there was very little that could rouse him until sunrise.

She had listened to the servers in the great hall, and ascertained that he had, as usual, been drinking. He had not seen her tonight, and that would put him in a foul mood, but by now, he would be asleep.

Gently, Taretha unlocked the door to Blackmoore's quarters. She let herself in, then closed the door as quietly as possible. Loud snoring met her ears. Reassured, she moved steadily toward her gate to freedom.

Blackmoore had boasted about this many months ago when he had been in his cups. He had forgotten he had told her about it, but Taretha remembered. Now, she went to the small desk and opened a small drawer. She pressed gently on it, and the false bottom came loose in her hand, revealing a tiny box.

Taretha removed the key and returned the box to the drawer, closing it carefully. She then turned toward the bed.

On the right side, a tapestry hung on the stone wall. It depicted a noble knight doing battle with a fierce black dragon defending a huge pile of treasure. Taretha brushed the tapestry aside and found the room's real treasure—a hidden door. As quietly as she could, she inserted the key, turned it, and opened the door.

Stone steps led down, into darkness. Cool air bathed her face, and a scent of wet stone and mold assaulted her nostrils. She swallowed hard, facing her fear. She did not dare to light a candle. Blackmoore slept deeply, but the risk was far too great. If he knew what she was doing, he'd have her flogged raw.

Think of Thrall, she thought. *Think of what Thrall has faced*. Surely she could overcome a fear of the darkness for him.

She closed the door behind her and was suddenly standing in a blackness so absolute she could almost feel it. Panic rose up in her like a trapped bird, but she fought it down. There was no chance of getting lost here; the tunnel led only one way. She took a few deep, steadying breaths, and then began.

Cautiously, she descended the steps, extending her right foot each time to search for the next one. Finally, her feet touched earth. From here, the tunnel sloped downward at a gentle angle. She recalled what Blackmoore had told her about it. *Got to keep the lords safe, m'dear,* he had said, leaning over her so she could smell his wine-scented breath. *And if there's a siege, well, there's a way we can be safe, you and I.*

It seemed to go on forever. Her fears battled with her mind for control. *What if it collapses? What if after all these years, it's blocked? What if I trip here in the darkness and break my leg?*

Angrily, Taretha silenced the voices of terror. Her eyes kept trying to adjust to the darkness, but with no light whatsoever, they only strained futilely.

She shivered. It was so cold down here, in the dark. . . .

After what seemed an eternity, the ground began to gradually slope upward again. Taretha resisted the urge to break into a run. She would be furious with herself if she lost control now and tripped. She pushed forward steadily, though she could not help but quicken her pace.

Was it her imagination, or was there a lightening of this dreadful darkness? No, she was not imagining it. Up ahead, it was definitely lighter. She drew closer and slowed. Her foot struck something and she stumbled forward, striking her knee and outthrust hand. There were different levels of stone . . . Steps! She reached out a hand, moving upward step by slow step until her questing fingers touched wood.

A door. She had reached a door. Another horrible thought seized her. What if it was bolted from the outside? Wouldn't that make sense? If someone could escape Durnholde by this route, someone else with hostile intentions might be able to enter the same way. It was sure to be locked, or bolted. . . .

But it wasn't. She reached upward and pushed with all her strength. Ancient hinges shrieked, but the door swung open, falling flat with a loud bang. Taretha jumped. It was not until she lifted her head up through the small, square opening, the light seeming to her eyes as bright as day, that she breathed a sigh of relief and permitted herself to believe it was true.

The familiar smells of horses, leather, and hay filled her nostrils. She was in a small stable. She stepped fully out of the tunnel, whispering softly and reassuringly to the horses that turned to look with mild inquiry at her. There were four of them; their tack hung on the wall. She knew at once where she must be. Near the road but fairly far from Durnholde was a courier station, where riders whose business could not be delayed changed exhausted mounts for fresh ones. The light came through chinks in the walls. Taretha carefully closed the trap door in the floor through which she had entered, and hid it with some hay. She went to the stable door and opened it, almost blinking in the full, blue-white light provided by the two moons.

As she had surmised, she was on the outskirts of the small village that encircled Durnholde, inhabited by those who made their living off tending to the needs of the fortress's inhabitants. Taretha took a moment to get her bearings. There it was, the cliff face she had, as a child, imagined to be so like a dragon.

Thrall would be waiting there for her in the cave, hungry and perhaps injured. Buoyed by her victory over the dark tunnel, Taretha raced toward him.

When he saw her running over the crest of the small hill, her slim figure silver in the moonlight, Thrall was hard-pressed not to let out a shout of joy. He contented himself with rushing forward.

Taretha froze, then lifted her skirts and ran toward him in return. Their hands met and clasped, and as the hood fell back from her tiny face he saw her lips were wide in a smile.

"Thrall!" she exclaimed. "It is so good to see you, my dear friend!" She squeezed the two fingers her own little hands could hold as tightly as she could and almost bounced with excitement.

"Taretha," he rumbled affectionately. "Are you well?"

The smile faded, then returned. "Well enough. And you? We have heard of your doings, of course! It is never pleasant when Lord Blackmoore is in a foul mood, but as it means that you are free, I have come to look forward to his anger. Oh. . . ." With a final squeeze, she dropped Thrall's hands and reached for the sack she had been carrying. "I did not know if you were wounded or hungry. I wasn't able to bring a great deal, but I brought what I could. I have some food, and some skirts I tore up for bandages. It's good to see you don't need—"

"Tari," Thrall said gently, "I did not come alone."

He signaled to his scouts, who had been waiting in the cave, and they emerged. Their faces were twisting into scowls of disapproval and hostility. They drew themselves up to their full height, folded their arms across their massive chests, and glared. Thrall watched her reaction carefully. She seemed surprised, and for a brief moment, fear flitted across her face. He didn't suppose he could blame her; the two outriders were doing everything they could to appear menacing. Finally, though, she smiled and strode up to them.

"If you are friends of Thrall, then we are friends also," she said, extending her hands.

One of them snorted in contempt and batted her hand away, not hard enough to hurt her, but enough to throw her slightly off balance. "Warchief, you ask too much of us!" one of them snapped. "We will spare the females and their young as you command, but we will not—"

"Yes you will!" Thrall replied. "This is the female who risked her life to free me from the man who owned both of us. She is risking her life again to come to our aid now. Taretha can be trusted. She is different." He turned to regard her fondly. "She is special."

The scouts continued to glare, but looked less certain of their prejudgment. They exchanged glances, then each took Taretha's hands in turn.

"We are grateful for what you have brought," said Thrall, switching back to human speech. "Rest assured, it will be eaten, and the bandages kept. I have no doubt that they will be needed."

The smile faded from Tari's face. "You intend to attack Durnholde," she said.

"Not if it can be avoided, but you know Blackmoore as I do. On the morrow, my army will march to Durnholde, prepared to attack if needed. But first I will give Blackmoore the opportunity to talk to us. Durnholde is the center of the camp controls. Break it, we break all the camps. But if he is willing to negotiate, we will not shed blood. All we want is to have our people freed, and we will leave the humans alone."

Her fair hair looked silver in the moons' light. She shook her head sadly. "He will never agree," she said. "He is too proud to think of what would be best for those he commands."

"Then stay here with us," said Thrall. "My people will have orders not to attack the women and children, but in the heat of battle, I cannot guarantee their safety. You will be at risk if you return."

"If I am discovered missing," Tari replied, "then that will alert someone that something is going on. They might find and attack you first. And my parents are still there. Blackmoore would take out his anger on them, I am sure. No, Thrall. My place is, and always has been, at Durnholde, even now."

Thrall regarded her unhappily. He knew, as she could not, what chaos battle brought. What blood, and death, and panic. He would see her safe, if he could, but she was her own person.

"You are courageous," said one of the scouts, speaking up unexpectedly. "You risk your personal safety to give us our opportunity to free our people. Our Warchief did not lie. Some humans, it would seem, do understand honor." And the orc bowed.

Taretha seemed pleased. She turned again to Thrall. "I know it sounds foolish to say, but be careful. I wish to see you tomorrow night, to celebrate your victory." She hesitated, then said, "I have heard rumors of your powers, Thrall, are they true?"

"I don't know what you have heard, but I have learned the ways of the shamans. I can control the elements, yes."

Her face was radiant. "Then Blackmoore cannot possibly stand against you. Be merciful in your victory, Thrall. You know we are not all like him. Here. I want you to have this. I've been so long without it, it doesn't feel right for me to keep it anymore."

She inclined her head and removed the silver chain and crescent pendant. Dropping it in Thrall's hand, she folded his fingers over it. "Keep it. Give it to your child, if you have one, and perhaps I may visit him one day."

As she had done so many months ago, Taretha

stepped forward and hugged Thrall as best she could. This time, he was not surprised by the gesture, but welcomed it and returned it. He let his hand caress her golden, silky hair, and desperately hoped that they would both survive the coming conflict.

She pulled back, reached up to touch his strong-jawed face, turned and nodded to the others, then turned and purposefully strode back the way she had come. He watched her leave with a strange feeling in his heart, holding her necklace tightly. *Be safe, Tari. Be safe.*

It was only when she was well away from the orcs that Tari permitted the tears to come. She was so afraid, so dreadfully afraid. Despite her brave words, she didn't want to die any more than anyone else did. She hoped Thrall would be able to control his people, but she knew that he was unique. Not all orcs shared his tolerant views toward humans. If only Blackmoore could be persuaded to see reason! But that was as likely as her suddenly sprouting wings and flying away from all of this.

Although she was human, she wished for an orc victory—Thrall's victory. If he survived, she knew the humans would be treated with compassion. If he fell, she could not be certain of that. And if Blackmoore won—well, what Thrall had experienced as a slave would be as nothing to the torment Blackmoore would put him through now.

She returned to the little stable, opened the trap door, and stepped down into the tunnel. Her thoughts were so full of Thrall and the coming conflict that this time the darkness bothered her hardly at all.

Taretha was still deep in thought when she ascended the stairs to Blackmoore's room and eased the door open.

Abruptly, dark lanterns were unshielded. Taretha gasped. Seated in a chair directly opposite the secret door was Blackmoore, with Langston and two rough-looking, armed guardsmen.

Blackmoore was stone cold sober, and his dark eyes glittered in the candlelight. His beard parted in a smile that resembled that of a hungry predator.

"Well met, my traitor," he said, silkily. "We've been waiting for you."

NINETEEN

The day dawned misty and foggy. Thrall smelled rain in the air. He would have preferred a sunny day, the better to see the enemy, but rain would keep his warriors cooler. And besides, Thrall could control the rain, if it came down to that. For now, he would let the weather do what it would.

He, Hellscream, and a small group of Frostwolves would go ahead. The army would follow behind. He would have preferred to utilize the cover provided by the trees, but an army of nearly two thousand would need the road. If Blackmoore kept scouts posted, then he would be alerted. Thrall did not remember such scouts from his time at Durnholde, but things were very different now.

His small advance party, armored and armed, moved steadily down the road toward Durnholde.

Thrall called a small songbird and asked it to look about for him. It came back in a few minutes and in his mind Thrall heard, *They have seen you. They are racing back to the keep. Others are moving to circle behind.*

Thrall frowned. This was quite well organized, for Blackmoore. Nonetheless, he knew his army outnumbered the men at Durnholde nearly four to one.

The bird, perched on one of his massive forefingers, waited. *Fly back to my army and find the old, blind shaman. Tell him what you have told me.*

The songbird, its body a golden yellow and black and its head bright blue, inclined its blue head and flew to execute Thrall's request. Drek'Thar was a trained warrior as well as a shaman. He would know what to do with the bird's warning.

He pressed on, feet steadily moving forward. The road curved, and then Durnholde in all its proud, stony glory loomed up before them. Thrall sensed a change in his group.

"Hold up the flag of truce," he said. "We will observe the proprieties, and it may prevent them from opening fire too soon. Before, we have stormed the encampments with ease," he acknowledged. "Now we must face something more difficult. Durnholde is a fortress, and will not be taken easily. But mark me, if negotiations fail, then fall Durnholde will."

He hoped it would not come to that, but he expected the worst. It was unlikely that Blackmoore would be reasonable.

Even as he and his companions moved forward, Thrall could see movement on the parapets and walkways. Looking more closely, he saw the mouths of cannons opening toward him. Archers took their positions, and several dozen mounted knights came cantering around the sides of the fortress to line up in front of it. They carried lances and spears, and halted their horses. They were waiting.

Still Thrall came. There was more movement atop the walls directly above the huge wooden door, and his heart sped up a little. It was Aedelas Blackmoore. Thrall halted. They were close enough to shout. He would approach no farther.

"Well, well," came a slurred voice that Thrall remembered all too well. "If it isn't my lil' pet orc, all grown up."

Thrall did not rise to the bait. "Greetings, Lieutenant General," he said. "I come not as a pet, but as a leader of an army. An army that has defeated your men soundly in the past. But I will make no move against them this day, unless you force my hand."

Langston stood beside his lord on the walkway. He couldn't believe it. Blackmoore was rip-roaring drunk. Langston, who had helped Tammis carry his lord to bed more times than he cared to admit, had never seen Blackmoore so drunk and still be able to stand. What had he been thinking?

Blackmoore had had the girl followed, of course. A scout, a master of stealth and sharp of eye, had unbarred the door in the courier's stable so she would be able to emerge from the tunnel. He had watched her greet Thrall and a few other orcs. He had seen her give them a sack of food, seen her *embrace* the monster, by the Light, and then return via the no-longer-secret tunnel. Blackmoore had feigned his drunkenness last evening, and had been quite sober when the shocked girl had walked back into his bedchamber to be greeted by Blackmoore, Langston, and the others.

Taretha had not wanted to talk, but once she learned that she had been spied upon, she made great haste to assure Blackmoore that Thrall had come to talk peace. The very notion had offended Blackmoore deeply. He dismissed Langston and the other guards, and for many paces outside his door Langston could still hear Blackmoore cursing and even the sound of a hand striking flesh.

He hadn't seen Blackmoore again until this moment, though Tammis had reported to him. Blackmoore had sent out his fastest riders, to get reinforcements, but they were still at least four hours away. The logical thing to do would be to keep the orc, who had after all raised the flag of truce, talking until help arrived. In fact, etiquette demanded that Blackmoore send out a small party of his own to talk with the orcs. Surely Blackmoore would give the order any moment. Yes, it was the logical thing to do. If the count was right, and Langston thought it was, the orcish army numbered over two thousand.

There were five hundred and forty men in Durnholde, of whom fewer than four hundred were trained warriors who had seen combat.

As he watched uneasily, Langston saw movement on the horizon. They were too far away for him to detect individuals, but he clearly saw a huge green sea begin to move slowly over the rise, and heard the steady, unnerving sound of drums.

Thrall's army.

Though the morning was cool, Langston felt sweat break out under his arms.

"Tha's nice, Thrall," Blackmoore was saying. As Thrall watched, disgusted, the former war hero swayed and caught himself on the wall. "What did you have in mind?"

Once again, pity warred with hatred in his heart. "We have no desire to fight humans anymore, unless you force us to defend ourselves. But you hold many hundreds of orcs prisoners, Blackmoore, in your vile encampments. They will be freed, one way or another. We can do it without more unnecessary bloodshed. Willingly release all the orcs held prisoner in the encampments, and we will return to the wilds and leave humans alone."

Blackmoore threw back his head and laughed. "Oh," he gasped, wiping tears of mirth from his eyes, "oh, you are better than the king's jester, Thrall. *Slave*. I swear, it is more entertaining to watch you now than it was when you fought in the gladiator ring. Listen to you! Using complete sentences, by the Light! Think you understand mercy, do you?"

Langston felt a tug on his sleeve. He jumped, and turned to behold Sergeant. "I've no great love for you, Langston," the man growled, his eyes fierce, "but at least you're sober. You've got to shut Blackmoore up! Get him down from there! You've seen what the orcs can do."

"We can't possibly surrender!" gasped Langston, though in his heart he wanted to.

"Nay," said Sergeant, "but we should at least send out men to talk to them, buy some time for our allies to get here. He *did* send for reinforcements, didn't he?"

"Of course he did," Langston hissed. Their conversation had been overheard and Blackmoore turned bloodshot eyes in their direction. There was a small sack at his feet and he nearly stumbled over it.

"Ah, Sergeant!" he boomed, lurching over toward him. "Thrall! Here's an old friend!"

Thrall sighed. Langston thought he looked the most composed of all of them. "I am sorry that you are still here, Sergeant."

"As am I," Langston heard the Sergeant mutter. Louder, Sergeant said, "You've been too long away, Thrall."

"Convince Blackmoore to release the orcs, and I swear on the honor that you taught me and I possess, none within these walls shall come to harm."

"My lord," said Langston nervously, "You recall what powers I saw displayed in the last conflict. Thrall had me, and he let me go. He kept his word. I know he's only an orc, but—"

"Y'hear that, Thrall?" bellowed Blackmoore. "You're only an orc! Even that idiot Langston says so! What kin' of human surrenders to an orc?" He rushed forward and leaned over the wall.

"Why'd you do it, Thrall?" he cried brokenly. "I gave you everything! You and me, we'd have led those greenskins of yours against th' Alliance and had all the food and wine and gold we could want!"

Langston stared, horrified. Blackmoore was now screaming his treachery to all within earshot. At least he hadn't implicated Langston . . . yet. Langston wished he had the guts to just shove Blackmoore over the wall and surrender the fortress to Thrall right now.

Thrall didn't waste the opportunity. "Do you hear that, men of Durnholde!" he bellowed. "Your lord and master would betray all of you! Rise up against him, take him away, yield to us, and at the end of the day you will still have your lives and your fortress!"

But there was no sudden stirring of rebellion, and Thrall supposed he couldn't blame them. "I ask you once more, Blackmoore. Negotiate, or die."

Blackmoore stood up to his full height. Thrall now saw that he held something in his right hand. It was a sack.

"Here's my answer, Thrall!"

He reached into the sack and pulled something out. Thrall couldn't see what it was, but he saw Sergeant and Langston recoil. Then the object came hurtling toward him and struck the ground, rolling to a stop at Thrall's feet.

Taretha's blue eyes stared sightlessly up at him from her severed head.

"That's what I do with traitors!" screamed Blackmoore, dancing madly on the walkway. "That's what we do with people we love who betray us . . . who take everything and give nothing . . . who sympathize with double-damned *orcs!*"

Thrall didn't hear him. Thunder was rolling in his ears. His knees went weak and he fell to the earth. Gorge rose in his throat and his vision swam.

It couldn't be. Not Tari. Surely not even Blackmoore could do such an abominable thing to an innocent.

But blessed unconsciousness would not come. He remained stubbornly awake, staring at long blond hair, blue eyes, and a bloody severed neck. Then the horrible image blurred. Wetness poured down his face. His chest heaving with agony, Thrall recalled Tari's words to him, so long ago: *These are called tears. They come when we are so sad, so soul sick, it's as if our hearts are so full of pain there's no place else for it to go.*

But there was a place for the pain to go. Into action, into revenge. Red flooded Thrall's vision now, and he threw back his head and screamed with rage such as he had never before experienced. The cry burned his throat with its raw fury.

The sky boiled. Dozens of lightning strikes split the clouds, dazzling the eye for a moment. The furious peals of crashing thunder that followed nearly deafened the men at the fortress. Many of them dropped their weapons and fell to their knees, gibbering terror at the celestial display of fury that so clearly echoed the wrenching pain of the orc leader.

Blackmoore laughed, obviously mistaking Thrall's rage for helpless grief. When the last peals of thunder died down, he yelled, "They said you couldn't be broken! Well, I broke you, Thrall. *I broke you!*"

Thrall's cry died away, and he stared at Blackmoore. Even across this distance, he could see the blood drain from Blackmoore's face as his enemy now, finally, began to understand what he had roused with his brutal murder.

Thrall had come hoping to end this peacefully. Blackmoore's actions had destroyed that chance utterly. Blackmoore would not live to see another sunrise, and his keep would shatter like fragile glass before the orcish attack.

"Thrall. . . ." It was Hellscream, uncertain as to Thrall's state of mind. Thrall, his chest still raw with grief and tears still streaming down his broad green face, impaled him with his glance. Mingled sympathy and approval showed in Hellscream's expression.

Slowly, harnessing his powerful self-control, Thrall raised the great warhammer. He began to stamp his feet, one right after the other, in a powerful, steady rhythm. The others joined him at once, and very faintly, the earth trembled.

Langston stared, sickened and appalled, at the girl's head on the ground thirty feet below. He had known Blackmoore had a streak of cruelty, but he had never imagined. . . .

"What have you done!" The words exploded from Sergeant, who grabbed Blackmoore and spun him around to face him.

Blackmoore began laughing hysterically.

Sergeant went cold inside as he heard the screams, and then felt the slight tremble in the stone. "My lord, he makes the earth shake . . . we must fire!"

"Two thousand orcs all stomping their feet, 'course the earth's going to shake!" snarled Blackmoore. He veered back toward the wall, apparently intent upon verbally tormenting the orc still further.

They were lost, Langston thought. It was too late to surrender now. Thrall was going to use his demonic magic, and destroy the fortress and everyone in it as retaliation for the girl. His mouth worked, but nothing came out. He felt Sergeant staring at him.

"Damn the lot of you noble-born, heartless bastards," Sergeant hissed, then bellowed, *"Fire!"*

*   *   *

Thrall did not even twitch when the cannons went off. Behind him he heard screams of torment, but he was untouched. He called on the Spirit of Earth, pouring out his pain, and Earth responded. In a clean, precise, direct line, the earth heaved and buckled. It went straight from Thrall's feet to the mammoth door like the burrowing of some giant underground creature. The door shuddered. The surrounding stone trembled and a few small stones fell, but it was more soundly built than the slapped-together walls of the encampments, and held.

Blackmoore shrieked. His world took on a very sharp focus, and for the first time since he had gotten himself drunk enough to order Taretha Foxton's execution he was thinking clearly.

Langston hadn't exaggerated. Thrall's powers were immense and his tactic to break the orc had failed. In fact, it had roused him to an even greater fury, and as Blackmoore watched, panicked and sick, hundreds . . . no, thousands . . . of huge, green forms flowed down the road in a river of death.

He had to get out. Thrall was going to kill him. He just knew it. Somehow, Thrall was going to find him and kill him, for what he'd done to Taretha. . . .

Tari, Tari, I loved you, why did you do this to me?

Someone was shouting. Langston was yapping in one ear, his pretty face purple and eyes bulging with fear, and Sergeant's voice was in the other, screaming nonsensical noises. He stared at them helplessly.

Sergeant spat some more words, then turned to the men. They continued to load and fire the cannons, and below Blackmoore the mounted knights charged the ranks of orcs. He heard battle cries and the clash of steel. The black armor of his men milled with the ugly green skin of the orcs, and here and there was a flash of white fur as . . . by the Light, had Thrall really managed to call white wolves to his army?

"Too many," he whispered. "There are too many. So many of them. . . ."

Again, the very walls of the fortress shook. Fear such as Blackmoore had never known shuddered through him, and he fell to his knees. It was in this position, crawling like a dog, that he made his way down the steps and into the courtyard.

The knights were all outside fighting, and, Blackmoore presumed, dying. Inside, the men who were left were shrieking and gathering what they could to defend themselves—scythes, pitchforks, even the wooden training weapons with which a much younger Thrall had honed his fighting skills. A peculiar, yet familiar smell filled Blackmoore's nostrils. Fear, that was it. He'd reeked of the stench in battles past, had smelled it on dead men's corpses. He'd forgotten how it had churned his stomach.

It wasn't supposed to be this way. The orcs on the other side of the now-shuddering gates were supposed to be his army. Their leader, out there screaming Blackmoore's name over and over again, was supposed to be his docile, obedient slave. Tari was supposed to be

here ... where was she, anyway ... and then he remembered, he remembered, his own lips forming
around the order that had taken her life, and he was
sick, right in front of his men, sick in body, sick in soul.

"He's lost control!" bellowed Langston inches from
Sergeant's ear, shouting to be heard over the sounds of
cannon, sword impacting shield, and cries of pain. Yet
again, the walls shuddered.

"He lost control long ago!" Sergeant shouted back.
"You're in command, Lord Langston! What would you
have us do?"

"Surrender!" Langston shrieked, without hesitation.
Sergeant, his eyes on the battle thirty feet below, shook
his head.

"Too late for that! Blackmoore's done us all in.
We've got to fight for it now until Thrall decides he
wants to talk peace again ... if he ever does. What
would you have us do?" Sergeant demanded again.

"I ... I ..." Anything resembling logical thought
had fled from Langston's brain. This thing called battle,
he was not made for it—twice now he had crumbled in
the face of it. He knew himself for a coward, and de-
spised himself for it, but the fact remained.

"Would you like me to take command of the defense of Durnholde, sir?" asked Sergeant.

Langston turned wet, grateful eyes to the older man
and nodded.

"Right, then," said Sergeant, who turned to face the men in the courtyard and began screaming orders.

At that moment, the door shattered, and a wave of orcs crashed into the courtyard of one of the most powerfully constructed fortresses in the land.

TWENTY

The skies seemed to open and a sheet of rain poured down, plastering Blackmoore's dark hair to his skull and making him slip in the suddenly slick mud of the courtyard. He fell hard, and the wind was knocked out him. He forced himself to scramble to his feet and continue. There was only one way out of this bloody, noisy hell.

He reached his quarters and dove for his desk. With trembling fingers, he searched for the key. He dropped it twice before he was able to stumble to the tapestry beside his bed, tear the weaving down, and insert the key into the lock.

Blackmoore plunged forward, forgetting about the steps, and hurtled down them. He was so inebriated that his body was limp as a rag doll's, however, and suffered only a few bruises. The light shining in the door from his quarters reached only a few yards, and up ahead yawned utter darkness. He should have brought a lamp, but it was too late now. Too late for so many things.

He began to run as fast as his legs would carry him. The door on the other side would still be unbolted. He could escape, could flee into the forest, and return later, when the killing was over, and feign . . . he didn't know. Something.

The earth trembled again, and Blackmoore was knocked off his feet. He felt small bits of stone and earth dust him, and when the quake ceased, he eased himself up and moved forward, arms extended. Dust flew thickly, and he coughed violently.

A few feet ahead, his fingers encountered a huge pile of stone. The tunnel had collapsed in front of him. For a few wild moments, Blackmoore tried to claw his way out. Then, sobbing, he fell to the ground. What now? What was to become of Aedelas Blackmoore now?

Again the earth shook, and Blackmoore sprang to his feet and began to race back the way he had come. Guilt and fear were strong, but the instinct to survive was stronger. A terrible noise rent the air, and Blackmoore realized with a jolt of horror that the tunnel was again collapsing right behind him. Terror lent him speed and he sprinted back toward his quarters, the roof of the tunnel missing him by a foot or two, as if it was following his path a mere step behind.

He stumbled up the stairs and hurled himself forward, just as the rest of the tunnel came down with a mighty crash. Blackmoore clutched the rushes on the floor as if they could offer some solidity in this suddenly mad world. The terrible shaking of the earth seemed to go on and on.

Finally, it ended. He didn't move, just lay with his face to the stone floor, gasping.

A sword came out of nowhere to clang to a stop inches from his nose. Shrieking, Blackmoore scuttled back. He looked up to see Thrall standing in front of him, a sword in his own hand.

Light preserve him, but Blackmoore had forgotten just how *big* Thrall was. Clad in black plate armor, wielding a massive sword, he seemed to tower over the prone figure of Blackmoore like a mountain towers over the landscape. Had he always had that set to his huge, deformed jaw, that . . . that presence?

"Thrall," Blackmoore stammered, "I can explain. . . ."

"No," said Thrall, with a calmness that frightened Blackmoore more than rage would have. "You can't explain. There is no explanation. There is only a battle, long in the coming. A duel to the death. Take the sword."

Blackmoore drew his legs up beneath him. "I . . . I . . . ."

"Take the sword," repeated Thrall, his voice deep, "or I shall run you through where you sit like a frightened child."

Blackmoore reached out a trembling hand and closed it about the hilt of the sword.

Good, thought Thrall. At least Blackmoore was going to give him the satisfaction of fighting.

The first person he had gone for was Langston. It had been ease itself to intimidate the young lord into revealing the existence of the subterranean escape tunnel. Pain had sliced through Thrall afresh as he realized that this must have been the way Taretha had managed to sneak out to see him.

He had called the earthquakes to seal the tunnel, so that Blackmoore would be forced to return by this same path. While he waited, he had moved the furniture angrily out of the way, to clear a small area for this final confrontation.

He stared as Blackmoore stumbled to his feet. Was this really the same man he had adored and feared simultaneously as a youngster? It was hard to believe. This man was an emotional and physical wreck. The vague shadow of pity swept through Thrall again, but he would not permit it to blot out the atrocities that Blackmoore had committed.

"Come for me," Thrall snarled.

Blackmoore lunged. He was quicker and more focused than Thrall had expected, given his condition, and Thrall actually had to react quickly to avoid being struck. He parried the blow, and waited for Blackmoore to strike again.

The conflict seemed to revitalize the master of Durnholde. Something like anger and determination came into his face, and his moves were steadier. He feinted left, then battered hard on Thrall's right. Even so, Thrall blocked effectively.

Now he pressed his own attack, surprised and a bit pleased that Blackmoore was able to defend himself and only suffered a slight grazing of his unprotected left side. Blackmoore realized his weakness and looked about for anything that could serve as a shield.

Grunting, Thrall tore the door off its hinges and tossed it to Blackmoore. "Hide behind the coward's door," he cried.

The door, while it would have made a fine shield for an orc, was of course too large for Blackmoore. He shoved it aside angrily.

"It's still not too late, Thrall," he said, shocking the orc. "You can join with me and we can work together. Of course I'll free the other orcs, if you'll promise that they'll fight for me under my banner, just as you will!"

Thrall was so furious he didn't defend himself properly as Blackmoore unexpectedly lunged. He didn't get his sword up in time, and Blackmoore's blade clanged off the armor. It was a clean blow, and the armor was all that stood between Thrall and injury.

"You are still drunk, Blackmoore, if you believe for an instant I can forget the sight of—"

Again, Thrall saw red, the recollection of Taretha's blue eyes staring at him almost more than he could

bear. He had been holding back, trying to give
Blackmoore at least a fighting chance, but now he
threw that to the wind. With the impassive rage of a
tidal wave crashing upon a seacoast city, Thrall bore
down on Blackmoore. With each blow, each cry of
rage, he relived his tormented youth at this man's
hands. As Blackmoore's sword flew from his fingers,
Thrall saw Taretha's face, the friendly smile that en-
veloped human and orc alike, and saw no difference between them.

And when he had beaten Blackmoore into a corner,
and that wreck of a man had seized a dagger from his
boot and shoved it up toward Thrall's face, narrowly
missing the eye, Thrall cried out for vengeance, and
brought his sword slicing down.

Blackmoore didn't die at once. He lay, gasping, fingers impotently clutching his sides as blood pumped
out in a staggering rush of red. He stared up at Thrall,
his eyes glazed. Blood trickled from his mouth, and to
Thrall's astonishment, he smiled.

"You are . . . what I made you . . . I am so proud . . ."
he said, and then sagged against the wall.

Thrall stepped out of the keep into the courtyard.
Driving rain pelted him. At once, Hellscream splashed
up to him. "Report," demanded Thrall, even as his eyes
swept the scene.

"We have taken Durnholde, my Warchief," said Hellscream. He was spattered with blood and looked ec-

static, his red eyes burning bright. "Reinforcements for the humans are still leagues distant. Most of those who have offered resistance are under our control. We have almost completed searching the keep and removing those who did not come to fight. The females and their young are unharmed, as you asked."

Thrall saw clusters of his warriors surrounding groups of human males. They were seated in the mud, glaring up at their captors. Now and then one would rally, but he was quickly put in his place. Thrall noticed that although the orcs seemed to want very badly to assault their prisoners, none did.

"Find me Langston." Hellscream hastened to do Thrall's bidding, and Thrall went from cluster to cluster. The humans were either terrified or belligerent, but it was clear who had control of Durnholde now. He turned as Hellscream returned, driving Langston in front of him with well-timed prods from his sword.

At once Langston dropped to his knees in front of Thrall. Vaguely disgusted, Thrall ordered him to rise. "You are in command now, I assume?"

"Well, Sergeant . . . yes. Yes I am."

"I have a task for you, Langston." Thrall bent down so that the two were face-to-face. "You and I know what sort of betrayal you and Blackmoore were plotting. You were going to turn traitor to your Alliance. I'm offering you a chance to redeem yourself, if you'll take it."

Langston's eyes searched his, and a bit of the fear left his face. He nodded. "What would you have me do?"

"Take a message to your Alliance. Tell them what has happened this day. Tell them that if they choose the path of peace, they will find us ready to engage in trade and cooperation with them, provided they free the rest of my people and surrender land—good land—for our use. If they choose the path of war, they will find an enemy the likes of which they have never seen. You thought we were strong fifteen years past—that is as nothing to the foe they will face on the battlefield today. You have had the good fortune to survive two battles with my army. You will, I am sure, be able to properly convey the full depths of the threat we will pose to them."

Langston had gone pale beneath the mud and blood on his face. But he continued to meet Thrall's eyes evenly.

"Give him a horse, and provisions," said Thrall, convinced his message had been understood. "Langston is to ride unhindered to his betters. I hope, for the sake of your people, that they listen to you. Now, go."

Hellscream grabbed Langston by the arm and led him to the stables. Thrall saw that, per his instructions, his people who were not occupied with guarding the humans were busily taking provisions from the keep. Horses, cattle, sheep, sacks of grain, bedding for bandages—all the things an army needed would soon be provided to the new Horde.

There was one more man he needed to talk to, and after a moment, he found him. Sergeant's small group of men had not surrendered their weapons, but neither were they actually using them. It was a standoff, with both orcs and humans armed, but neither particularly desirous of escalating the conflict.

Sergeant's eyes narrowed warily when he saw Thrall approach. The circle of orcs parted to admit their Warchief. For a long moment, Sergeant and Thrall regarded one another. Then, faster than even Sergeant had credited him for, Thrall's hand was on Sergeant's earlobe, the golden hoop firmly between his thick green fingers. Then, just as swiftly, Thrall released him, leaving the earring where it was.

"You taught me well, Sergeant," Thrall rumbled.

"You were a fine student, Thrall," Sergeant replied cautiously.

"Blackmoore is dead," said Thrall. "Your people are being led from the fortress and its provisions taken even as we speak. Durnholde stands now only because I will it to stand." To illustrate his point, he stamped, once, on the ground, and the earth shook violently.

"You taught me the concept of mercy. At this moment, you should be very glad of that lesson. I intend to level Durnholde in a few moments. Your reinforcements will not arrive in time to be of any help to you. If your men will surrender, they and their families will be permitted to leave. We will see to it that you have food and water, even weapons. Those who do not surrender will die in the rubble. Without this fortress and its knights to protect the camps, we will find it easy to liberate the rest of our people. That was always my only goal."

"Was it?" Sergeant said. Thrall knew he was thinking of Blackmoore.

"Justice was my goal," said Thrall. "And that has, and will be, served."

"Do I have your word that no one will come to harm?"

"You do," said Thrall, lifting his head to look at his people. "If you offer us no resistance, you will be permitted to walk out freely."

For answer, Sergeant tossed his weapon to the muddy earth. There was a silence, and then the armed men did likewise. The battle was over.

When everyone, human and orc, was safely away from the fortress, Thrall called upon the Spirit of Earth.

This place serves nothing good. It housed prisoners who had done no wrong, elevated evil to great power. Let it fall. Let it fall.

He spread out his arms and began to stamp rhythmically on the earth. Closing his eyes, Thrall remembered his tiny cell, Blackmoore's torture, the hatred and contempt in the eyes of the men he had trained with. The memories were shockingly painful as he sifted through them, reliving them briefly before letting them go.

Let it fall. Let it fall!

The earth rumbled, for the final time in this battle.

The sound was ear-splitting as the mighty stone buildings were pulverized. Earth churned upward, almost as if it was eating the fortress. Down it came, the symbol to Thrall of everything he had fought against. When the earth was at last still, all that was left of the mighty Durnholde was a pile of rocks and jagged pieces of wood. A huge cheer went up from the orcs. The humans, haggard and haunted, simply stared.

In that pile, somewhere, was Aedelas Blackmoore's body.

"Until you bury him in your heart, you won't be able to bury him deep enough," came a voice by his side. Thrall turned to look at Drek'Thar.

"You are wise, Drek'Thar," said Thrall. "Perhaps too wise."

"Was it good to kill him?"

Thrall thought before answering. "It needed to be done," he said. "Blackmoore was poison, not just to me, but to so many others." He hesitated. "Before I killed him, he . . . he said that he was proud of me. That I was what he had made me. Drek'Thar, the thought appalls me."

"Of course you are what Blackmoore made you," Drek'Thar replied, surprising and sickening Thrall with the answer. Gently, Drek'Thar touched Thrall's armor-clad arm.

"And you are what Taretha made you. And Sergeant, and Hellscream, and Doomhammer, and I, and even Snowsong. You are what each battle made you, and you are what you have made of yourself . . . the lord of the clans." He bowed, then turned and left, guided by his attendant Palkar. Thrall watched them go. He hoped that one day, he would be as wise as Drek'Thar.

Hellscream approached. "The humans have been given food and water, my Warchief. Our outriders report that the human reinforcements will shortly be closing in. We should leave."

"In a moment. I have a duty for you to perform." He extended a closed fist to Hellscream, then opened it. A silver necklace with a crescent moon dropped into Hellscream's outstretched hand. "Find the humans called Foxton. It is likely that they have only now learned about their daughter's murder. Give this to them and tell them . . . tell them that I grieve with them."

Hellscream bowed, then left to do Thrall's bidding. Thrall took a deep breath. Behind him was his past, the ruin that had once been Durnholde. Before him was his future, a sea of green—his people, waiting, expectant.

"Today," he cried, raising his voice so that all could hear, "today, our people have won a great victory. We have leveled the mighty fortress Durnholde, and broken its grasp on the encampments. But we cannot yet rest, nor claim that we have won this war. There are many of our brothers and sisters who yet languish in prisons, but we know that they will soon be free. They, like you, will taste what it is to be an orc, to know the passion and power of our proud race.

"We are undefeatable. We will triumph, because our

cause is just. Let us go, and find the camps, and smash their walls, and free our people!"

A huge cheer rose up, and Thrall looked around at the thousands of proud, beautiful orcish faces. Their mouths were open and their fists were waving, and every line of their large bodies spoke of joy and excitement. He recalled the sluggish creatures in the encampment, and felt a stab of almost painful pleasure as he allowed himself to realize that he had been the one to inspire them to these heights. The thought was humbling.

A profound peace swept over him as he watched his people cry his name. After so many years of searching, he finally knew where his true destiny lay; knew deep in his bones who he was:

Thrall, son of Durotan . . . Warchief of the Horde.

He had come home.

ABOUT THE AUTHOR

Award-winning author Christie Golden has written eighteen novels and sixteen short stories in the fields of science fiction, fantasy, and horror. She launched the TSR Ravenloft line in 1991 with her first novel, the highly successful *Vampire of the Mists*, which introduced elven vampire Jander Sunstar. Golden followed up *Vampire* with *Dance of the Dead* and *The Enemy Within*.

Golden has written six *Star Trek: Voyager* novels, including the popular *Dark Matters* trilogy, and has been involved in three other *Star Trek* projects. Her latest "trek" was a special addendum to the novelization of the *Voyager* finale *Endgame*, in which she takes the characters in new directions. Golden will continue writing *Voyager* novels even though the show is off the air, and she is eager to explore the creative freedom that gives her.

Though best known for tie-in work, Golden is also the author of two original fantasy novels from Ace Books, *King's Man & Thief* and *Instrument of Fate*, which made the 1996 Nebula Preliminary Ballot. Under the pen name Jadrien Bell she wrote a historical fantasy thriller entitled *A.D. 999*, which won the Colorado Author's League Top Hand Award for Best Genre Novel of 1999.

Golden lives in Denver, Colorado, with her portrait-artist husband, two cats, and a white German shepherd. Readers are encouraged to visit her at her Web site, www.christiegolden.com.